Things Are Different Here
and other stories

Rod Michalko

INSOMNIAC PRESS

Library and Archives Canada Cataloguing in Publication

Michalko, Rod, author
Things are different here / Rod Michalko.

Short stories.
Issued in print and electronic formats.
ISBN 978-1-55483-188-3 (softcover).
--ISBN 978-1-55483-202-6
(HTML)

I. Title.
PS8626.I19T45 2017   C813'.6   C2017-903987-3
C2017-903988-1

The publisher gratefully acknowledges the support of the
Canada Council for the Arts and the Ontario Arts Council.

Printed and bound in Canada

Insomniac Press
520 Princess Avenue, London, Ontario, Canada, N6B 2B8
www.insomniacpress.com

THE CANADA COUNCIL | LE CONSEIL DES ARTS
FOR THE ARTS | DU CANADA
SINCE 1957 | DEPUIS 1957

ONTARIO ARTS COUNCIL
CONSEIL DES ARTS DE L'ONTARIO

For Austin Clarke

For Tanya Titchkosky

For Lynn Manning

Acknowledgements

Many people have made this book possible. Thanks to Mike O'Connor of Insomniac Press for showing interest in the manuscript and deciding to publish it. Rinaldo Walcott put me in touch with Mike; I owe Rinaldo several shots of bourbon for this. I have had several editors in the past but none better than Dan Varrette of Insomniac Press. He truly enriched my writing and, for this, I am grateful. I am especially indebted to Sarah Hoedlmoser, who has the amazing capacity for transcribing my Dictaphone mumblings while providing invaluable editorial suggestions. My long-time friend Heather Berkeley has supported this book project from its inception. For reading the stories and discussing them with me, I am grateful. I owe her several glasses of Chardonnay. I am also thankful for the friendship of Radek Puky, Eve Haque, Abdi Osman, Mary-Jo Nadeau, Steve Tufts, Jim Cosgrave, and many other Toronto friends, too many to name here. The entire crew of Kilgour's has given me countless evenings of fun, love, and lively conversation, and this has been a source of inspiration. I am also influenced by echoes from Nova Scotia, heard in the voices of Dan Ahern, Dan & Judy MacInnes, and others. For this, I am grateful. The feature story in this collection is set in Manchester, UK, where several people have influenced the writing of this book. I owe much to Rebecca Lawthom, Dan Goodley, and their two daughters, Ruby and Rosa. Their love has been a source of energy and support. The encouragement of Neil Carey, Murry Murat, Jenny Fisher, and a host of other Mancunians also inspired and guided me along the way. The late Lynn Manning, a brother in blindness, taught me to understand blindness as a calling for artistic expression. I sincerely hope that I have represented Lynn's sense of "profound blindness" well in the following pages. Tanya Titchkosky, as she always does, provided me with unending support and encouragement. Right from the beginning, she's been fascinated by my blindness and has not let me forget that I owe blindness the thoughtful and creative expression it deserves. For pushing me to publish the following stories, I am grateful. I owe her several bottles of red wine. Finally, I am very grateful to the late Austin Clarke. He taught me to write fiction. On so many occasions, I sat in his kitchen, where Tanya would read drafts of my stories aloud and Austin would follow his own copy and teach me to "show, not tell" what I meant. He taught me to bring blindness to life through dialogue. Sitting in his house, surrounded by books, great food, booze, and interesting people, remains one of the most profound influences in my life and in the writing of these stories. I dedicate this book to his memory.

Contents

Explain Yourself

"You know what I'm getting tired of?"

"No, Jason. What are you getting tired of?"

"Hey. Don't be a smartass. It's about you."

"I'm not being a smartass. What are you saying? You getting tired of me?"

"I'm always tired of you, Matthew, but here's what I'm *really* getting tired of."

"What?"

"All right. I'm getting *really* tired of explaining you. Yeah, Matty, *you*—explaining you."

"Explaining me! What are you talking about?"

Jason tied his shoes. He removed the combination lock from the locker door and put it in his backpack. He stood and slammed his locker shut.

"Come on, Matty. Get moving. Let's grab a coffee, and I'll tell you about it."

"I'm hurrying. I'm hurrying. That bicep routine was tough, man. I'm a little slow. I'm hurtin'."

"Aww, muffin. I'll wait."

Jason and Matthew had been working out in this gym for the past three years or so. They liked it— Gold's Gym, on St. Clair West. They liked this

Toronto neighbourhood too. It was predominantly Italian, back in the day. Now, though, it was changing; it was becoming Caribbean. Jason and Matthew enjoyed this neighbourhood.

They always worked out at about the same time, around nine in the morning. This meant that they could beat the lunch crowd that spilled onto St. Clair West at around noon every day. There were great Italian restaurants, and now great Caribbean ones, on the street. They ate lunch only rarely after a workout, but they always had coffee. What could be better? Italian coffee and Caribbean coffee—nothing better.

Jason and Matthew left the locker room and moved toward the stairs that would take them down through the lobby and out onto the street.

"I got it, Jason. I got it."

"You sure?"

"Yeah. There. I got the banister. You go. See you at the bottom."

"Good."

Matthew found the first stair with his white stick. He grasped the banister firmly with his left hand and made his way down the twenty-two stairs.

"Okay, man," Matthew said as he reached the bottom. "Let's go."

"All right, Matty. Here's my arm."

Jason and Matthew came out of Gold's Gym and onto a sun-filled street. It was that time of year in Toronto—early May and not yet oppressively hot. The air was fresh despite the busyness of St. Clair West. There was a lot of traffic, including noisy streetcars, but even this didn't take away from the freshness of a late spring morning. The outdoor markets were bustling—people talking, discussing who knows what and doing so through the animation of Italian and the sweetness of Caribbean accents.

Matthew loved St. Clair West. On this street he felt a rich sense of *being* somewhere, of being a part of something. People almost always spoke to him. They called him "Matty." The people in the markets and the cafés, and even the people on the street, knew his name. Sometimes he felt as though he were the resident blind guy—their personal blind guy. Matthew liked this feeling; he had been living in this area for about three years now, and he felt very good about being a part of things.

He'd met Jason in one of the local bars shortly after he'd moved to the neighbourhood. He'd come into the bar and was greeted by Jason almost immediately.

"You okay? Need some help? Wanna sit at the bar? Table? What? I'm Jason. You?"

Matthew didn't experience someone as straightforward as Jason very often. Blindness just wasn't one of those ordinary things, after all. People were usually a little nervous. Not Jason, though.

"Here. Here. My hand. Shake. Shake. What's your name, man?"

And so a great friendship began.

"So, what are you thinking? Marcello's? Jolly Café?"

"No, no. Come on, Matty. Nice day like this—not too cold, not too hot—best thing: Julietta's. Great patio!"

"Okay. Good. Right on my street."

"All right, man. Don't get all excited. It's just that it's got a great patio. Your street is *irrelevant*."

"Okay. Let's go, Jason."

Matthew took Jason's arm and together they made their way to Café Julietta. It didn't take long. Julietta's was only two blocks from Gold's Gym. Even in this short distance, though, a couple of people greeted them in that teasing way that showed affection.

"Hey, you guys slumming?" came a man's voice from the patio of the Jolly Café.

"'Course. Why else would we be here walkin' on the street?" came Jason's response.

"Hey, Matty, stop slummin' with the guy."

"I know. But I couldn't find no one else to guide me."

Walking, jamming with others, laughing, they made their way down the street to Julietta's.

"You gonna eat somethin'?"

"No. Too early."

"What are you talking about, Matty? 'Too early.' It's eleven-thirty, man."

"Yeah. I know. But I don't wanna eat till one-thirty or so. If I eat now, well, then I'm gonna be hungry about five, five-thirty."

"So? You can't have a snack?"

"No, Jason. I can't have a snack."

"So, dude, you watching your figure now?" Jason said, laughing.

"Watchin' the figure, man. Watchin' the figure." He laughed.

"I'm not eatin' either."

"You watchin' your figure, too?" Matthew said, still laughing.

"'Course I'm watching my figure. Gotta look good. Gotta look good."

"Look what the wind blew on my patio. How you guys doin'?"

"Dom! What up, man?"

"Ain't much, ain't much, Jason. Matty, you okay?"

"Yeah, Dom. What's shaking?

"What's shaking? What's shaking? Business is bad. I got you two guys here drinkin' nothing but coffee—no meals, no booze. How am I supposed to make money? What's shaking?"

"Dominic. Dominic," Matthew said. "You got the best patio on the street here. I dunno what you do with all your money."

"Yeah, Dom, what do you do with all that cash of yours?"

"Yeah, yeah. All my cash. I use it to support guys like you—you know, coffee, 'Just coffee, Dom.'"

All three of them were laughing. Matthew lived half a block down the street from Julietta's and spent a lot of time at the café. Jason, who lived a block over, did the same. This was one of their favorite haunts.

"Okay," Jason said. "We don't got all day, Dom. So couple coffees."

"Okay, Mr. Big Shot. Cappuccino? Americano? Same as usual?"

"Yeah," Matthew said. "Thanks, Dom."

"Back in a sec."

"Cool," Matthew said. "So, Jason, what's this about explaining me? What are you getting tired of?"

Jason leaned toward him, ignoring his question. "Hey, Matty," he said, lowering his voice.

"What?"

"There's, uh, at the other end of the patio." Jason was almost whispering now. "I mean, she's gotta be the most beautiful woman I've ever seen."

"So, you can see. Big deal. Quit bragging."

"Hey, I'm not bragging. Just lettin' you know what you're missin'," Jason said, laughing.

"Thanks, man. Thank God I can always count on you," Matthew said, laughing too. "But what's up with this explaining stuff?"

"Oh. Yeah. Right," Jason said, leaning back in his chair. "Remember, at the end? 'Member you got on the bike and—"

"Yeah. And you—you went over to the elliptical?"

"Yeah. Yeah. So this guy—this guy on the one next to me—he's on the next machine."

"Yeah?"

"He looks at me and he says, 'That your buddy over there on the bike?'"

"Really?"

"Yeah, dude. Really. The guy says, 'That your buddy?' I figured what the hell, but, you know, I say, 'Yeah.'"

"What did he say?"

"Okay, you two deviants, here we go. Americano...right there, Matty. Right there. By your hand. Right there. Cappuccino. You got sugar. You got nice milk—heated up. Okay?"

"Perfect," Matthew said. "Thanks, Dom."

"You guys need anything, you call me."

"Dom," Jason said. "You good man."

"Yeah, yeah. Enjoy."

"Okay. So what'd he say, Jase?"

"Oh, yeah. He says to me, like, as if it's any of his business, he says, 'So can your buddy see anything or...?'"

"What did you say?"

"I told him no, Matty. I said, 'Nothing, zero, blanko.'"

"Blanko?" Matthew said, laughing. "What the hell is that?"

"You know, *blanko*," Jason said. "I told him blanko, zilch. I didn't want to tell him 'bout all those lights of yours, know what I mean?"

"Yeah," Matthew said. "You're right. Buncha

lights. You're right. That's really tough to explain."

"No, no. That's not the explaining part I'm getting tired of."

"It isn't? What then?"

"Here it is, Matty," Jason said. "Okay. He asks.... All right, buncha people asked me this already."

"What buncha people? Asked you what?"

"They say—you know, they say, 'What's the story? What's the scoop with the blindness?'"

"Ohhh..." Matthew said, the light dawning on him. "They wanna know why I'm blind, how I lost my sight. Ohhh...."

"Finally. You get it. I'm gettin' really tired of tellin' people stuff. I'm gettin' tired of explainin' you. That's it, Matty. No more."

"What are you going to do?" Matthew said, laughing. "What are you gonna tell people? Actually, what *do* you tell people? What'd you tell the guy at the gym?"

"What do you mean 'what'd I tell him'?" Jason said. "I make up shit. That's what I tell 'em."

"You would," Mathew said, laughing harder now. "You would make up some shit."

"'Course I make up some shit. I'm not gonna tell them the truth. I don't even know the truth."

"So what do you tell 'em?"

"Never mind what I tell 'em. I don't wanna explain you anymore. You explain yourself. By the way, what the hell happened to your eyes?"

In the three years he had known him, Jason had never asked about his eyesight. How did you lose it? Were you always blind? Jason never asked him these kinds of questions. He was asking them now, though, and Matthew found it funny.

"What're you laughing at, Matty?"

"Uh, nothin' really. Just thinking about, you know, what a great 'hood, good people, you know."

"That's true, man," Jason said. "That's true."

"I gotta get more coffee. You? See Dom anywhere?"

"No. When I do, I'll order a couple more."

"Great. Okay, Jason, what'd you tell that guy? What'd you tell him happened to my eyes?"

"Wait, wait, wait. Dom!" Jason shouted. "Couple more, and make it quick."

"You'll get it when you get it," Dom said, and went back into the café.

"Thanks," Matthew said.

"No prob, man."

"Okay, Jase, what's the scoop?"

"What's the scoop? Whaddaya mean 'what's the scoop'?"

"You know what I mean. What did you tell that guy about my eyes?"

"Oh," Jason said. "You mean that guy in this great 'hood?"

"Yeah, yeah. 'That guy in this great 'hood.' Stop fucking around, Jason, and tell me what you told him."

"Okay," Jason laughed. "Okay."

"You probably told him something really goofy," Matthew said. "Didn't you?"

"What am I s'posed to tell him?" Jason said. "I dunno what happened to your eyes. So if I'm gonna tell someone what happened, well, I'm gonna have to make some stuff up. Right?"

"Yeah," Matthew agreed. "But I know you. You probably made up something really, I mean, *really* ridiculous."

"Ridiculous!" Jason said with feigned surprise. "Not me."

"Right. So what'd you tell him, Jase?"

"Hang on a sec," Jason said. "Here comes Dom."

"Good," Matthew said.

"Dom! Finally! Where'd you go? Tim Hortons? Did you go there for the coffee?"

"Don't be a smarty, Jason. Keep it up and I *will* get you a coffee from Tim Hortons."

"Don't talk like that," Jason said.

"Yeah," Dom said. "There you go, Matty. Your Americano...and some fresh milk. You got enough sugar?"

"Yeah. I'm good, Dom. Thanks."

"Jason...cappuccino. There you go. You guys happy? Need anything else?"

"No. We're good, man," Matthew said.

"All right. You let me know."

Matthew added a couple of sugar lumps and some milk to his Americano. He began stirring.

"Want some more milk? Looks like you could

use some more milk."

"Thanks. I got it."

Matthew methodically placed the spout of the little milk container on the edge of his cup. Using his other hand to secure the cup, he began to slowly pour milk into his Americano.

"Is it comin' out?"

"Yeah," Jason said. "Keep going...a little more."

"How's that?"

"Good," Jason said. "Looks good to me."

Matthew replaced the milk container on its saucer and began stirring again. "Mmm. Good." He loved Americanos, and he especially loved the ones Dom made.

"Okay, man," Matthew said. "So what'd you tell the guy?"

"Okay, Matthew, but you gotta understand...."

"Understand what?"

"Relax, Matty," Jason said, tapping him on the forearm. "Don't freak out. Relax. No biggie. Relax."

"Yeah. Relax. Easy for you to say. But who knows what the hell you're gonna say?"

"Yeah, well, I just made up some stuff. You know, I dunno what happened to your eyes. So I figure it's not important, otherwise you'd tell me. Am I right?"

"Yeah. I guess."

"Well, guess or not," Jason continued, "I figure, if it's important and I gotta know, you would tell me."

"True. But what—?"

"So I figure...since you don't tell me, well, then I got the right—you know, I got the right. Someone asks me, I got the right to tell them, well, whatever."

Whatever, Matthew thought and smiled. He knew that whatever Jason told the man about what happened to his eyesight, it would fall somewhere between outrageous and hysterically funny—maybe even both. Matthew leaned in toward Jason. "What'd you tell him? What'd you tell him, Jase?"

"Relax, man," Jason said, laughing. "Relax. It's no big deal."

"I know. I'm just curious. So what the hell d'you tell him?"

"You don't have to yell."

"I'm not yelling, Jason."

"Yeah, you are. All right. All right, I'll tell you."

"Okay. Good."

"Then you're gonna relax? Right?" Jason was enjoying himself. He knew that he might be going a little far with Matthew, but *what the hell*, he thought. It was all in good fun. If Matty was getting a little freaked, *well*, Jason thought, *that's his problem.*

Jason told all sorts of stories about Matthew's eyesight. People in the neighbourhood knew they were friends. Jason was proud of this. Over the past three years or so, Matthew had become a very good friend, but there was something about being proud of this friendship that Jason didn't quite understand. He sometimes wondered why he felt proud that Matthew was not only his friend but also his *blind* friend. What was wrong with him? Blind, not blind—what's the diff? What's the big deal? And yet, Jason knew it was. Being friends with Matthew, a blind guy, made him proud. Jason wasn't sure, though, if he was proud of this.

Oh, whatever, he thought. People did ask him about Matthew. Jason smiled as he thought of all the different things he'd said about Matthew's blindness. "No, nothing," he remembered telling one person. "It's all just total blackness. Total darkness." "It's just white and grey, like clouds," he remembered telling another person. Jason had told several stories about how Matthew lost his sight, too. Hitting his head on the side of the swimming pool when he was trying out for the Canadian Olympic diving team was one of them. Being knocked out by a roundhouse kick to the head during a pro mixed martial arts match was another. All the stories were kinda macho, though. Oh well. He had fun with it, and that was the important thing.

"Jason!" Matthew raised his voice.

"What?"

"Quit daydreaming and tell me what you told that guy."

"Okay, okay. Keep your shirt on."

"Just tell me."

"Okay, Matty. But you gotta remember...."

"Remember what?"

"Remember we were in the gym. That's what."

"Okay."

"Okay, so this dude, Matty—honest, the guy is fucking jacked, man. I mean, he's huge. And he's lookin' at you. So I give a little glance over your way, and I see, you know, you're jacked too."

"What's this got to do with anything?"

"Keep your shirt on. Okay, so you're jacked. But you look like, uhhh, in better shape than this guy. You're jacked, but you're a little wiry. Know what I mean? You're in your early thirties. I mean, you look tough."

"I'm not tough."

"I know, I know. But you *look* tough. Sooo, I take advantage of this."

"What do you mean?"

Jason leaned in. He looked left and then right as though checking to see whether anyone was within earshot. He dropped his voice and said, "I told the guy—I told him you're an ex-Navy SEAL."

"*What?* Jason, you told him *what?*"

"Hey, hey, hey...."

"*Ex-Navy SEAL?*"

"Matty. Keep your voice down. The patio's filling up. Lunch crowd."

"Okay, okay. But why did you tell him that?"

"It's like this—this guy.... I mean, this guy looks over at you...."

"Yeah."

"This guy—I mean it, Matty—this guy is like a gym rat. He's huge! And he's thick. I mean, he's thick like two planks."

"So?" Matthew said.

"So. Okay. The guy says—I mean, he looks at you and says, 'Your buddy there,' he says. 'He looks good—good arms. Really ripped.' See what I mean?"

"No," Matthew said. "What's that got to do with anything?"

"'Cause this guy is all, like, into, you know, good arms—shit like that. But listen to this, Matty. The guy says to me, I mean, really says, 'So what happened to your buddy? Did he get hit in the head? Is he a hockey player? Did he get hit with a puck? Or what?'"

"Really?" Matthew said.

"Honest to God," Jason said. "That's what the guy said."

"Man."

"So get it, Matty? This is a macho dude, so I give him what he wants."

"Whaddaya mean 'what he wants'?"

"Ahh c'mon, man. You know what I mean. He wants you to lose your sight, you know, in a macho way. You look macho, so you have to be a blind macho man. You can't just be a blind man. Get it?"

"Yeah. I get it."

"So I give the dude *blind macho man*. I tell him that you were in the Navy SEALs and in special ops in Iraq."

"You're crazy," Matthew said.

"Maybe," Jason continued, "but it's fun. So I

tell the guy you were in some kind of firefight and you lost your eyesight. You should have *seen him*, Matty. The dude's mouth falls open and he says, '*You're kidding!*' I said, 'No. No shit. Really.' The guy is, like, totally impressed. See? I give him what he wants."

Matthew and Jason began laughing.

"No kidding," Jason continued. "I tell the guy, 'Three years ago,' I said. 'Three years ago, my friend moves to Canada from the States 'cause he doesn't like the way vets are treated in America.'"

"How do you think of this stuff?" Matthew said, laughing almost hysterically now.

"I dunno. It just comes to me. I just give these people exactly what they want. Tell 'em exactly what they think. Who knows? Maybe this guy—maybe, Matty, you never know—maybe later today, next week, next month, maybe he rethinks it and realizes how fucked up he is. Then maybe he changes."

"Look at you go, Jase. You're just goin' around the world, doin' good."

"Yeah, well, someone's gotta do it."

"Jason."

"Yeah?"

"Sometimes, you know, man, sometimes, well, you're a lot smarter than you look."

"You too, Matty. You too. Gimme the fist."

They fist-bumped and Matthew stood.

"Where you going, man?" Jason said.

"Gotta pee. Be right back."

Jason and Matthew always took the table just to the right of the side door whenever they came to Café Julietta. This table was almost always available. As Matthew made his way through the door and into the café, he wondered about that. He thought that maybe Dominic had something to do with it. This made him smile.

Matthew entered the café and turned left. In four or five steps, he would be at the stairs that led down to the bathroom.

"You okay, Matty?"

"I'm good, Dominic. Good. Thanks."

"Okay," Dominic said.

Dominic always said the same thing. He always asked Matthew if he was okay as he approached the stairs. Matthew thought about that as he dried his hands on some paper towel. *Every time*, Matthew thought. *How did Dominic do it? How was he always looking?* Matthew smiled and began to make his way back to the patio.

"Matty. You're back."

"Yeah."

"My turn," Jason said as he stood and headed to the bathroom.

Matthew located his coffee cup. He took a sip. The coffee was cold. He wondered whether he and Jason would have another coffee before leaving. Matthew thought he might like to stay, whether Jason did or not.

"Excuse me," a man said, putting his hand on Matthew's shoulder. "Sorry to bother you."

The man's touch startled him a little. "Pardon?" Matthew said.

"Listen, no offense, 'kay?"

"No, no," Matthew said. "It's okay. What's up?"

"So, you were special ops, eh?"

"Yes. I was," Matthew said, touching the man's hand.

Studio Apartment in D Major

It was small, but he liked it. Three hundred fifty square feet—a studio, they called it. Not a bachelor, a studio. He guessed that "bachelor" was out of date, and he understood why. Kind of a sexist term, he thought. Studio—studio apartment—that's a better name.

Small, but he could afford it...almost eight hundred a month. At least there was a bathroom with a shower, and there was even a little kitchen: fridge, stove, the whole nine yards. His last place—now there was a dump. Four hundred bucks a month. Just a room. The bathroom was down the hall. Everyone on his floor, the second, and on the third floor, too, had to share the bathroom, including the shower. Five rooms! Five people! Three on his floor, two on the one above—all sharing one lousy bathroom. And no fridge, no stove. Microwave, that's all—he'd had just a microwave. Thank God his buddy had loaned him that little fridge; it was little, but it was a fridge.

Queen Street East—that dump was on Queen Street East, not Toronto's trendy Queen Street West, not that dump. Queen Street East. It was near Queen on Lewis Street. His room was on the second floor of a three-story house. It wasn't just his room that was a dump, the whole house was. And not just on the inside, the outside too. The whole thing was a dump. Chunks were missing out of the concrete steps that led to the front door, there was peeling wallpaper in the front entrance and on the walls that guided the stairs up to the second and third floors, and...the smell, a funny mixture of cheap booze, cheap perfume, and some other sort of smell that he always thought was bad cooking emanating from somewhere on the main floor. A dump.

And yet he'd managed. He got to know some of the staff and regulars in the coffee shops, cafés, and bars up and down Queen Street East. A few of them were even in a similar position as he was: aspiring musicians, and even a few actors.

He thought of these things as he walked through his new Toronto neighbourhood: the Annex. His apartment building was on Walmer Road, just a little north of Bloor Street. It wasn't one of those huge high-rises that seemed to be popping up all over Toronto. It was ten stories, a building and a location he could easily manage. The super was great, and he got along with all the other tenants he'd met so far. A lovely studio apartment. He loved it. Bathroom, shower, fridge, stove—everything. It had everything.

And he thought of this, too, as he walked west on Bloor Street. Late afternoon in mid-September, walking west on Bloor Street, getting more acquainted with the shops, the cafés, the bars. Today, late Friday afternoon, he was exploring the north side of Bloor.

He guided his white stick in a gentle right-to-left, left-to-right movement in front of him. He didn't really need it; he had enough vision—if seven or eight percent could be understood as enough—where he didn't need the assistance of a white stick to get around. But in the late afternoons of mid-September, he couldn't always count on the lighting. The sun began setting earlier this time of year, and he was walking due west, right into a sinking sun, a sun that looked him in the eye, a sun that penetrated whatever remaining vision he had, a sun that, despite the bright light it cast, removed almost all of what little sight he had. That was where the white stick came in handy.

"No," Jeff was saying. "I saw you from across the street, so I just ran over to say hi. You know, say 'how you doing?'"

"Yeah. Great," Marcus said, smiling and laughing a little. "I was just coming up to the light, you know, on Brunswick there, and I was really focusing, uh, trying to figure out if it was red or what."

"Sorry about that," Jeff said, joining Marcus in his nervous laugh. "I should have come up to you slower. Give you a chance to know I'm there. Sorry."

"No, no, no. No prob. Glad you came over. And

this is pretty cool. What did you call this place?"

"By the Way café," Jeff said.

"Cool. I like this place."

Jeff had done what so many people did, or so it seemed to Marcus. Suddenly...he was right there! A loud *"Marcus!"* was accompanied by a friendly tap, or, at least, what was intended as so, on Marcus's shoulder. "How are you!" Jeff's friendly voice, or, at least, what he had intended to be so, continued.

There they were—Marcus and Jeff—standing on Bloor Street, waiting for the light on Brunswick Avenue to turn in their favour. Marcus, though, had been standing there for some time—how long, he wasn't sure. That sun, that mid-September, late-afternoon sun; that sun that warmed the mid-September air so that the fast approaching coolness of autumn retreated ever so slightly; that sun, that friendly sun that made everyone on Bloor Street that afternoon seem a tiny bit happier than usual; but that sun reminded Marcus that it did have another side. It was difficult to call this "other side of the sun" its dark side, but there was something dark about it. It did, after all, enter Marcus's eyes, and not in that gentle way that everyone else on Bloor Street had noticed that mid-September late afternoon. It entered Marcus's eyes with a swift penetrating brilliance that drove all but a tiny slice of sight from them, leaving...well, leaving a kind of darkness—not like that of the night but a bright darkness with only a sliver of residual vision.

This sun—this penetrating, mid-September,

late afternoon sun—was different from what Marcus called "cut sun." That was a whole different ball game. Cut sun toyed with his vision. Cut sun could make an appearance at any time, in any season—autumn, summer, all of them. It had no seasonal discrimination.

The only thing that cut sun needed to make an appearance was an erratic shade. The shade created by a building that blocked the sun out, for example, or by a cloud, was not the kind of shade that cut sun looked for. It needed the shade created by trees or by buildings with uneven lines in its architecture. It needed the sunlight popping in and out, cutting through the shade, creating a sensation that Marcus was convinced was the inspiration for strobe lighting.

Cut sun cut through his vision (hence the name) but not in the way penetrating sun did. Instead, it gave Marcus the sensation of endless slices of sunlight that cut their way through endless slices of shade. It distracted his vision more than removed it. Cut sun gave Marcus a light show that made it nearly impossible for him to move with any confidence.

Today featured that clear, penetrating sun so characteristic of a mid-September late afternoon. And it wasn't Marcus's intention to walk in a westerly direction for too much longer. In fact, he was waiting at the corner of Bloor and Brunswick, figuring out traffic flows—both vehicular and pedestrian—that would permit him to cross over to the south side of Bloor. From there, his plan was to walk one more block west, knowing that at the end of that block, and after fighting that clear, penetrating sun, was Kilgour's, a bar that was quickly becoming his local. He would pop in there for a couple of beers, maybe even some chicken wings, talk to the staff and the regulars, and then head home. Who knew? he thought. Maybe he'd spend the better part of the evening there.

And then...Jeff.

"Glad you had time for a coffee," Jeff said. "Were you headed somewhere? Gotta be somewhere?"

"No, uh, just checking out the 'hood. You know. Nice spot, this By the Way café."

"Right. You haven't lived in this neighbourhood all that long."

"Yeah, into my second month. Moved in, uh, beginning of August."

"That's right," Jeff said. "And I met you—what was that?—oh, yeah, just after the Labour Day weekend. A Thursday. Remember?"

"I do. At the Tranzac. I remember. It was, ah, bluegrass—Hound's Tooth, good band."

"Yeah. They're there every Thursday night. You've been back since?"

"No," Marcus said, sounding as though he were choosing his words carefully. "I've been out of town for a week, but I'm definitely going back. Maybe next Thursday."

"I've been back a couple times. They're good; I really enjoy them. Oh, you know what?"

"What?"

"There was another reason I wanted to talk to you." Jeff's voice sped up a little.

"Oh?"

"Yeah. Actually, I was on my way home."

"Yeah."

"To pick up my guitar. Then I'm headed to the Tranzac. You know, same place where, uh, the bluegrass was."

"Really? You playing there tonight, Jeff?"

"A little, yeah. Every second Friday night, they have—they call it a 'jam.'"

"Oh, yeah?"

"Yeah. Bunch of us. Well, three or four of us. We get our guitars, and we meet over there and jam. They set up mics. I mean, the Tranzac does. And usually a couple of us sing a little. And jam. Just jam."

"Sounds great," Marcus said.

"Yeah. So I was thinking, you know, maybe you want to grab your guitar and come by. You know, join us for a little jamming. You're not booked anywhere, right? You're not playing anywhere tonight?"

"No," Marcus said slowly.

Truth be told, Marcus hadn't been booked anywhere, at least not in Toronto. Not since that gig in Grossman's Tavern on Spadina Avenue about a month ago. Still, there was that two-week stand at that great blues bar on Rue St-Denis in Montreal, Bistro à Jojo. He had just returned from there a week ago—actually, last Sunday to be precise. But all last week, nothing, and prospects didn't look good for the next two weeks. *At least I have those three nights at Hugh's Room in a couple of weeks*, Marcus thought. *Thank God. At least I have that.*

"So...you wanna do some jamming tonight?" Jeff persisted.

"Yeah. Don't see why not. I'll just head back to my place, grab a guitar, and join you. The Tranzac—just a little south of Bloor on Brunswick, right?"

"Yeah. I'm gonna get my guitar too. If you want, I can wait on the corner—just across the street there, on Brunswick there—and meet you. If you want, we can head over to the Tranzac together."

"Sounds good, Jeff. Here, I'll just pay for these coffees and we can head out."

It's only been, what, three, four months? Marcus reminded himself. He had moved into his Queen Street East room on May 1st. It was September 14th. Four and a half months. He had been in Toronto for the past four and a half months. *That's not too awful long*, Marcus reminded himself...again.

All the way from Vancouver, more than halfway across the country, Marcus had made the move. He had been thinking about it for quite a while, almost two years. And then one day he'd made up his mind. Sometime last spring, he had made up his mind. Move to Toronto. *This will definitely advance your career.* He was certain of that.

Marcus was convinced, and so were others in Vancouver, that there were more opportunities for blues artists in Toronto than there were in Vancouver. He wasn't as convinced now. Not that he was dejected. Far from it. After all, he'd landed several gigs: a few times at Grossman's Tavern, a place he really liked; a couple of times on the patio of Lola's in Kensington Market—those were good; he especially liked Clinton's Tavern on Bloor Street West; three times more on College Street, at Free Times, wasn't bad either—not his favourite but not bad.

Marcus had a plan, though. Not that it was working out all that well, at least so far, but he did have a plan that he brought with him from Vancouver. It was simple: move to Toronto, get to know the blues scene, get to know a number of musicians, and, this was the crux of the plan, form a blues band.

He wasn't an idealist. At least he didn't think so. He didn't think it would be "no prob" to form a band soon after he arrived in Toronto. He was more realistic than that. He knew how long it took to meet musicians, to get to know them, to get to know their style, their strengths, their weaknesses; it took a while to get in sync with one another. Marcus knew this.

He also knew that he had left a really great group of musicians back in Vancouver. Leaving the band wasn't easy, of course. Actually, it was difficult—very difficult. They were a good band, very popular in Vancouver and surrounding areas. The problem was that, with the exception of Marcus, the band members were perfectly happy having day jobs and playing music on the weekends. This didn't present any difficulty for the band, and it certainly didn't lead to any animosity. The source of the difficulty was Marcus. He had decided to make blues his full-time occupation. It wasn't for them, they'd said, but "you need to give it a shot" was the way the drummer had put it. And "give it a shot" Marcus did.

"I like this place," Marcus said. "It's got a nice, calm vibe, and I like the acoustics; they're good."

"Yeah. I know what you mean."

"Sorry?" Marcus said. "I didn't get your name."

"Oh. It's Jeanine. And you're...?"

"I'm Marcus." He reached his hand across the table to his left.

"Hi," she said, as they shook hands. "Great to meet you."

"You too," Marcus said. "You play guitar?"

"No," Jeanine said. "Keyboards, mostly. I also sing a little. You know, mostly backup vocals. You? Do you play?"

"Yeah. Guitar. You gonna play tonight?"

"I'm not sure. I only come here—I mean, not every time. You know, not every second Friday. But sometimes. Sometimes I come here. So I don't know. I'll see. They do have a piano here, so I don't know. Maybe I'll play a little. Who knows? Maybe someone will sing and I'll do some backup. We'll see. You playing?"

"I don't know," Marcus said. "I came here with, uh, Jeff. He told me about these jams."

"Oh, right. Jeff."

"Yeah," Marcus continued. "I don't know where he went to. I don't know. I think he's talking to someone somewhere. Anyway, he told me about this jam, and I figured, you know, what the hell, let's see what's going on. So I grabbed my guitar and came down here with Jeff. So we'll see."

"You want another beer?" Jeanine asked.

"Yeah. Okay. But let me get it." Marcus reached for his wallet.

"No, no. I got this one. You get the next one."

And she was up and walking toward the bar. *Cool—she's cool*, Marcus thought. If nothing else, at least he met a cool woman. That was worth the trip here to the Tranzac. And who knows? Maybe he'll hear some good blues and maybe even play some himself. What he really wanted, though, was to play and sing some blues with Jeanine. He thought that would be really cool.

"Here you go. I'll put it right in front of your right hand. Okay?"

"Yeah. Perfect."

"There's quite a few people here," Jeanine said as she returned to her seat at the table to the left and just in front of Marcus.

"Yeah," Marcus said. "Sounds like almost a roomful, is it?"

"Pretty much. Pretty much. Hey, Marcus...?"

"Yeah?"

"Uh," Jeanine began slowly, "I mean, please don't be offended, but...."

"I won't," Marcus said cheerfully. "I won't."

"Okay. Well, I noticed you coming in here with Jeff, and you had this." She touched Marcus's white stick as it lay folded on the table between them. "So that means—sorry, I mean...that means, uh, you're blind, right?"

"I am," Marcus said, laughing and reaching out to touch her hand. "Don't be offended. I'm blind. No big deal. Actually, I'm what's called, believe it or not, legally blind."

Jeanine joined Marcus in his laughter and put her hand, the one Marcus wasn't touching, on top of his hand, making a sort of "Marcus hand sandwich": her hand, his hand, her hand. She then removed the top hand of the sandwich and said, *"Legally blind?* What the fuck is that?"

Marcus continued to laugh and removed the middle of the sandwich. He said, "That means I won't get arrested by the sight cops."

Jeanine jacked up the intensity of her laugh and said, "Sight cops! That's too cool. But wouldn't it be great if there were such a thing? Sight cops!

"I know!" Marcus said, turning up the intensity of his own laugh. "They could wear, you know, big mirrored aviator glasses. Wouldn't that be way too cool?"

Jeanine was now wrapped up in the irony of their conversation. "Yeah," she said, waving her hands in excitement. "Right. And then—listen to this—their billy clubs, you know, their—what do you call those things?"

"Batons?"

"Yeah. Batons. Well, they could be—!" Her laughter nearly exploded over the table between them. "White sticks! White canes! You know, like this big," she said, putting her hand on Marcus's folded white stick. "Wouldn't that be *hilarious*?"

"No shit!" Marcus said, returning the explosion of laughter to her side of the table. "Okay. But listen. What about—I mean, if a sight cop was going to give out a ticket, you know, for being illegally blind"—he was now speaking between gasps of laughter—"I mean, would the ticket be in Braille?"

"Good question," Jeanine said, echoing Marcus's manner of speaking. "'Cause— imagine this—if the ticket was, I mean, if it was in Braille, well, and if the sight cop gave it to someone who was being *illegally* blind, that would prove it! Get it?"

"Yeah. I get it. The guy, the dude—the criminal—what's that...what do they call someone who does a crime? You know, on those cop shows. What are they called?"

"Oh," Jeanine said, adopting a more serious attitude. "Bad guys. The perp. Something like that."

"Right. If the bad guy—you know, the perp—said he was innocent but couldn't read the ticket because it was in Braille, then they got him! Busted."

"Freeze!" Jeanine said, pointing her hand and maneuvering it to resemble a gun. "Book him, Danno!"

People had often broached the topic of his blindness, but never in this way. No other time was it this creative, and never with laughter. Not like this. Laughter! He and Jeanine actually laughed. They made up a story about the "sight police" and, well, laughed. No getting away from it. They laughed.

Marcus was feeling quite relaxed, quite at home, sitting there in the Tranzac Club. The venue was small enough for him to get a good sense of the configuration of the room, and, of course, the company was great. Jeff had joined them at the table, and the conversation changed from the sight police to music but not before Jeff asked about their laughter.

"I heard you from the next room," Jeff said. "What the hell was so funny?"

"Oh. Nothing really," Jeanine said. "Marcus here was just explaining how he was legal and not criminal. Right, Marcus?"

"That's right," Marcus said, laughing and looking at Jeanine in a conspiratorial way, which started her laughing as well.

"What's with you guys?" Jeff said. "Criminal? What are you talking about?"

"Well, apparently," Jeanine began, slowly controlling her laughter, "it turns out—and I just learned this now—that there's two ways to be blind: legal and illegal."

"Oh," Jeff said. "And I suppose, Marcus, you're legal. Right?"

"Yup. Above board. Legally blind."

Jeanine's laughter spilled over the table as though she had swallowed something the wrong way. "Yeah," she said between gasps of laughter, "the sight cops got nothin' on him. *Nothin'.*"

"*Sight cops?*" Jeff said.

"Yeah," Marcus said. "Believe it or not—I know it's hard to believe—but there's some people who say they're blind—"

"And they're not!" Jeanine interrupted, continuing to laugh.

"You guys are crazy," Jeff said. "Forget the criminals. You wanna play some music?"

"Are we gonna start?" Marcus asked. "Sounds like it could be fun."

"Especially if you're not a criminal," Jeff said.

"Yeah. I was just telling Jeanine, uh, you know—like I was telling you a couple weeks ago— I was just explaining what being legally blind meant."

"Oh," Jeff said. "You mean that ten percent thing. Right?"

"Yeah."

"What ten percent thing?" Jeanine asked.

"I thought I told you," Marcus said. "Didn't I?"

"I don't remember. Did you?"

"I don't know. I forget. Anyway, if you have less than ten percent vision, then you're blind—you know, legally."

"Oh." Jeanine nodded her head as though she understood. "So...ten percent. Huh! That means...so it means that you can be blind and still see. Right?"

"Right," Marcus said.

"Well, that's the weirdest fucking thing I've ever heard. Cheers," Jeanine said, holding her glass up.

"Speaking of playing a little blues," Jeff said.

"Who's speaking of playing blues?" Jeanine said.

"No one. But I wanna change the topic, you know, from this legally blind stuff to the blues."

"Maybe it's the same topic," Marcus said.

"What do you mean?" Jeanine asked.

"Well," Marcus explained, "you know, blind, suffering, the blues—it's a perfect fit. Blindness and the blues—can't get better than that."

"Great," Jeff said, laughing. "That means I'm on the same topic. So, Jeanine...."

"Yeah?"

"You wanna play some piano? Some of us are gonna play guitar and—hey, Marcus?"

"What?"

"You wanna sit in? I mean, I don't know, maybe you could sing something. You know, we might know it, or if it's your own stuff, maybe we can jam. What do you think?"

"Wow!" Jeanine said. "You sing too? I saw you when you were coming in. You were carrying a guitar. But you sing too?"

"Yeah," Marcus said. "I cover a lot of stuff, but, uh, I've written some."

"Great!" Jeanine exclaimed. "You wanna play? I'll play piano. I'd love to do some covers with you. And then, uh, you know, maybe we could try, you know, try to do some of the stuff you wrote."

"Maybe," Marcus said. "It would be nice to do stuff with other people again. I mean, since I've been in Toronto...."

"How long have you been here?" Jeanine asked.

"About four months."

"From where? Where'd you move from?"

"Vancouver."

"Vancouver! You moved here? From beautiful Vancouver? From no winter? Just wait a couple of months; you're going to wish you'd never moved."

"Ah," Jeff interjected, "he's gonna love it. Just wait. You're gonna start playing a lot, Marcus, and...you'll see. You're gonna love it here."

"Yeah. I hope so," Marcus said.

"Me too," Jeanine said. "What did you do in Vancouver?"

"Played music. You know, played a lot of the local blues clubs, other places. I had a little blues band."

"Really?" Jeanine said. "So what made you pick up and move to T.O.?"

"There's more blues action out here, I heard— and, uh, Montreal is closer. I love the blues scene there."

"I guess you know about Grossman's and also places in Kensington Market, right?" Jeanine said.

"Yeah, I played there a few times. They're good places."

"Man," Jeanine said. "You're gonna have to let me know the next time you play."

"I will."

"Hey, you guys," Jeff interrupted, "I'm just gonna go check and see if everything's ready."

Marcus was glad that he had agreed to come to the Tranzac with Jeff. He liked the people. Jeanine was a lot of fun—lively and interesting. Marcus liked that. He looked in her direction and, surprising himself a little, wondered what sort of keyboard player she was and found himself looking forward to hearing her play.

Marcus knew what Jeff was like on the guitar; Jeff had invited him to his apartment a couple of times and they jammed a little. Marcus remembered that on one of those occasions, a friend of Jeff's—John? Dave? Marcus couldn't remember his name—was also there, and the three of them jammed. John, or Dave, or whatever his name was, Marcus remembered, was very good; he would make a great lead guitarist. And now he was wondering about Jeanine, about how good she was at the piano. This was what surprised him a little and what made him feel a little bad. Marcus liked Jeanine and was disappointed in himself; he didn't want to, but he found himself thinking of Jeanine in...in what? In practical terms. That's how he was thinking of her—practically. *Not good*, Marcus said to himself. *Not good.*

"Good to meet you. Rick, is it?" Marcus said as he held out his hand.

"Yeah, Rick. Marcus, right?"

"Yeah."

"Good to meet you, too," Rick said.

That was all of them now—Marcus and Jeff, both on guitar; Jeanine on piano with a mic; and Rick playing drums, playing the Tranzac house drum kit. As far as house drum kits went, this one wasn't too bad, Rick said, although he didn't like the "kicker" much.

"It's not really a smooth action," Rick said to Marcus as he sat at the drum kit, trying to get the bass drum to sound "smooth," as he put it.

"Yeah," Marcus said. "It sounds a little stiff."

"A little?" Rick said, laughing. "It's like no one's played this for about a hundred years."

"Don't laugh!" they heard Jeanine chime in. "This piano needs tuning."

"Doesn't sound too bad. That middle C octave could use a little work, though."

"Yeah," Jeanine said. "You're right. Not too

bad. It'll do."

"What do you guys want to do?" Jeff said.

"I don't know," Jeanine said. "But the D sounds good here. You guys want to do 'Stand by Me' in D?"

"Sounds good," Rick said, still working the kicker.

"I'm good with that," Jeff said. "Marcus, you okay with that? You wanna sing?"

"Sure, what the hell. Jeanine, you wanna to do some harmony? You wanna do the kind of thing that Buddy and Tracy did with 'Ain't No Sunshine'? Remember?"

"Oh, yeah. That's great. But, hey, why don't we just do 'Ain't No Sunshine'? You know, cover those two."

"Good with me," Marcus said. Jeff and Rick echoed their approval. "Wanna do a little keyboard intro?" Marcus asked Jeanine. "Kind of give us a tempo and then Rick can kick the rhythm in. That okay with you guys?"

Everyone gave their approval, and Jeanine began to play the opening bars of "Ain't No Sunshine" in D Major.

"You're amazing, Jeanine!" Marcus said.

They were standing at the bar after their set, she sipping white wine and he a pint of beer. Their set went well at the Tranzac on that late Friday afternoon—early evening, really. Those who were there applauded appreciatively and loudly. There were even calls of "Encore!" and "More!" Jeff and Rick were especially impressed with Marcus and Jeanine. There were high-fives among the four of them during the applause, and "Wow! I didn't know you guys were *that* good!" was the sentiment flowing from Jeff and Rick. They were actually surprised.

Of course, Jeff had heard both of them play before, and Rick had heard Jeanine, but not together and not in front of an audience of thirty, forty people. What's more, although they had heard Jeanine on the piano before, she had merely been "playing around" during those times, just playing a few notes before whichever band was about to play. And although Marcus had jammed with Jeff in his apartment a couple of times, tonight was different. Jeanine and Marcus had taken their music to a whole new level, Jeff and Rick thought.

Jeff knew that Marcus and Jeanine had played down to him at certain points during their set. He couldn't follow all of the diminished chords and progressions that the two of them were playing. Still, they had allowed him to play along with them—tag along is how Jeff thought of it. And yet he wasn't angry or disappointed—a little jealous, maybe—okay, maybe a little disappointed, too. But, man, could they play!

"That was something else, huh?" Jeff said, as he unplugged his guitar.

"No shit," Rick said. "Where'd this Marcus guy

come from? I mean, like, we're talking pro."

"Yeah," Jeff explained. "He had a blues band in Vancouver and decided to come to T.O. You know, better music scene and all that."

"Oh, yeah. Right. Well, he's pretty fucking good. Jeanine's great on the keyboard, too, eh? Marcus got a band here? I mean, in T.O.?"

"I don't think so. Not that I know. He's been doing a lot of solo stuff—Grossman's and like that."

"Did you tell him about Jazz Bistro? You know, the, uh, blues night—Wednesday night?"

"No," Jeff said. "Forgot. I gotta mention that to him."

"Good," Rick said.

"Hey, Rick?"

"Yeah?"

"Hey, man, you sounded pretty fucking good yourself on the drums. I'll tell you that."

"Ah, don't be crazy. Come on, Jeff, let's grab a beer."

"You guys are amazing!" Jeff said when he and Rick joined the others at the bar.

"Thanks, Jeff," Jeanine said.

"Yeah," Marcus said. "Thanks. But you two guys are pretty damn good, too. Excuse me. Whatever these two want—on my tab, okay?"

"You got it," the bartender said.

"I couldn't keep up with you guys," Jeff said.

"You were fine," Jeanine said.

"Yeah," Marcus said. "You were good."

"Yeah right," Jeff laughed.

"No. Seriously," Marcus continued. "I think we were playing some shit over you. But you laid some nice rhythm down. I mean, you were playing good rhythm. I was just fucking around, you know, noodling a bunch of stuff. But, jeez, Jeff, you laid down a good rhythm cover. You really did."

"He's right," Jeanine agreed. "I was just playing around, you know, following Marcus. Didn't you hear me? I was folding in all my classical training. Just having fun."

"Good thing you guys were doing covers," Rick said, laughing. "I knew the drumming to them, so thank God. I don't know what I would have done if you guys started playing, you know, some of your own stuff."

"You were good, Rick," Marcus said. "Man, that was fun."

"Hey, Marcus," Jeff said.

"What's up?"

"You got some of your own shit? I mean, those couple times you were at my place—you were playing some of the stuff that's yours. I mean, some stuff you wrote, right?"

"Yeah," Marcus said. "Just fooling around. But it would be fun to try it with you guys sometime."

"Really?" Jeanine said. "You serious?"

"Yeah," Marcus said. "We could...well, maybe we could find a place. You know, rent a rehearsal place or something. Maybe we could work on a few songs and find somewhere to play them. I don't know, maybe Grossman's."

"Hey!" Rick said. "I know. What about the Jazz Bistro?"

"What?" Marcus asked.

"The Jazz Bistro," Rick repeated.

"Oh, right," Jeff said. "You mean on Victoria Street there? Yeah, don't they have a blues night or something like that, on Thursdays or...?"

"On Wednesdays," Rick said excitedly. "Wednesday evenings. You go there, and there's a bunch of people playing. So you go there. You sign up. I don't know how you do it, but we can find out. Anyway, you take turns, you know, you take turns playing. Plus you get to meet a lot of people. A lot of blues artists. And some of them are really good."

"I know where you mean," Jeanine said. "I've been there a couple of times—not to play or anything like that. I just went with a couple of friends to have a couple drinks, something to eat, catch some blues, you know. It was good. Only thing is— you know what was funny about that place?"

"Funny?" Rick said.

"Yeah," Jeanine continued. "Funny. They were all white! Everyone. Even the staff and the servers and like that. Everyone was white! Can you be- lieve it?"

"Well," Jeff said slowly, "it's not like we're not white."

"I know," insisted Jeanine. "But, I mean, it's a blues place. You'd think—I mean, you'd think some- body would be black. I mean, come on. It's the blues."

And so arrangements were made and rehearsals began.

The Jazz Bistro scheduled them to play a three-song set. Jeanine continued to insist that "white blues"—well, that's just not blues. They made arrangements to get an electric keyboard, a drum kit, and guitars, including amplifiers, to the Jazz Bistro.

The minivan taxi disgorged them in front of the Jazz Bistro on Victoria Street. Jeanine, Marcus, Jeff, and Rick—all four of them—spilled out of the minivan, laughing and talking excitedly as though being dropped off by a soccer mom at the community centre. They stood on the sidewalk in front of the venue and gathered themselves. They looked at the bar and at one another with an unspoken understanding: They were about to play their first gig together. Nerves guiding them, they entered together.

"Jeanine," Marcus said with urgency in his voice.

"What is it?"

"The lighting! I need your arm."

Jeanine smiled. She said, "Well, at least we have a blind blues guy.... Legal too."

The Blended Curb

Eli was pretty sure that he was at the curb. He couldn't see the curb, after all, and all he had was that "fucking white cane," that white stick. That's what he had to rely on to know things, to know whether he was at the curb or not.

He was at the curb. Eli kept telling himself that.

He had made that right turn from the corner of the building, and in twelve or fifteen steps, he would reach the curb. Eli needed to walk straight—don't veer, even slightly, either left or right; walk straight. If he didn't, he would miss the curb.

Eli moved. His white stick, with its familiar rhythm, took him toward the curb.

In a few steps, Eli felt the sidewalk tilting forward slightly, tilting toward the curb. So far, so good. He hadn't touched anything with his white stick, except the sidewalk. No object, no person. Nothing was making him veer.

The sidewalk tilted downward and blended into the curb. That's what they called it—a blended curb—and it was a problem. Eli didn't like it very much. Good for people in wheelchairs, but not for him.

Eli now slowed his pace. *Yeah, there's the blend*, he thought.

I hate this, Eli said to himself. *There's the traffic, up close. Fucking blend.* It's hard to tell where the sidewalk.... *Fucking wheelies*, he thought.

"You're right. There's gotta be a way," Tony said.

"Well, yeah, there's gotta be a way," Eli said. "But you guys—you guys always come first. Done the curb for you fucking rolling stockers and *theeeeen* worry about how we blind dudes gonna find the curb with our white sticks."

"Yeah, well, we rolling stockers...we're *waaaaay* more important than you blind dudes."

"Yeah. We'll see who's more important when I stick this cane of mine right in your ass. Den we see where you go."

"Think so? This chair of mine, man? It's titanium. It's *fast*! I'll go by you in a flash so quick you won't even *seeeee* me."

They both laughed.

"Fuck," Tony said. "Gimme five, Eli."

Eli raised his hand, palm out. Tony reached across the table and gave him five. They were still laughing.

Eli and Tony had met two years ago. They were both enrolled in the same sociology class at the University of Chicago. Eli always sat in the front row, and since that was the only place Tony could park his wheelchair, so did he.

"Excuse me," Tony had said after the first class. "I'm in a wheelchair. Be out of your way in a sec."

"Oh, sorry, man. I'll wait. Lemme know."

"No worries. Okay, there you go."

"Cool."

"Uh, you got another class now? I mean, you got somewhere to go now?"

"Nah, man," Eli said. "I'm gonna go grab a coffee or somethin'."

"Want company? Like, can I join you?"

"Yeah. Cool."

"Great. Let's go."

"Hey, man. Maybe...maybe I just hang onto your wheelchair here and...and you do your rolling thing, and I come right behind you with this white stick."

"Great! That'll give people something to stare at."

"Yeah. No shit. All right, let's roll."

He shouldn't have stepped off the curb, and he knew it. He shouldn't have decided so quickly, and he knew this too. And yet you had to make quick decisions sometimes, didn't you?

No one around him thought he had made a quick decision; no one thought he was acting quickly. Everyone around him thought he'd made a mistake; they thought he messed up; they thought he stepped off the curb at the wrong time.

They thought all of these things, but they didn't think he acted quickly.

"Hey, Tony. You good? Time for another beer, man? You see her? She around?"

"No...no...wait! Got her. Okay, got two more comin'."

Eli and Tony had been in this bar before; this was their third time. They liked it—for the same reasons and for different ones, too.

The bar was small. There were only eight tables in their favourite place to sit. There were more tables at the back, but Eli and Tony never sat there. There was too little room between the tables, and Tony had some difficulty maneuvering his wheelchair between them. There was more room between the tables up front, and Tony was more comfortable there.

Eli, too, liked sitting at the front. He had a sense of this area, not something that came easy to him. Four tables along one wall, four more on the opposite wall, and about an eight- to ten-foot space forming a nice negotiable hallway between the two rows of tables. Knowing this gave Eli a good sense of the shape of the room. *See*, Eli often said to himself and sometimes to others, *can't know the room—how big, how small, what shape it is—can't know nuthin'. Just know the little space where you sittin'. Can't know nuthin' else.* In this bar, though, Eli had a good sense of the room, up front. This made him feel good, and he could relax, as he was doing now.

The first time Eli and Tony had come into the bar, Tony located a table very near the bathroom. He was thrilled that he could roll into the bar. No stairs, wide doorway. Not every bar in Chicago was like that. But this bar—this bar was "wheeeeelchair wicked," as Tony had put it. And, as if that wasn't enough, there was plenty of room between the tables, and he could easily wheel his titanium chair right up to the table. Both of them liked the bathroom, too. No one thinks of the bathroom when they come into a bar. Eli and Tony both knew this. No one thinks of it until.... *No one give a shit*, Eli often said to himself and sometimes to others. *No one even think about the bathroom. He gotta be blind or a gimp or some kinda crip 'fore you even think 'bout the bathroom.*

Eli and Tony always tried to get the same table, and, so far, all three times, they had. It was the first table. *Come in through the side door*, Eli said to himself. *Follow the wall on the left 'til it and the carpet come to an end. Move forward, gettin' by the five- or six-foot space on the left, hit another wall, two more steps*—boom—*the table*. It was perfect. Eli loved getting in and out of this bar.

All three times, Eli had sat in the same chair. He sat there now. The end of the table was against the wall, and his chair was only about a foot from it. He could relax. The empty chair next to him, on his right, was great too. He could pull it out slightly and put his backpack on it. Sometimes he would put his arm on the back of the chair and lean back, relaxing, looking cool, *just like dem sighties*. Even better, there was a nice little corner where the end of the table met the wall. This was perfect too. Eli could stand his white stick right up in this snug little corner. His stick was there now, a foot away from his left hand. He could touch it whenever he wanted to.

Tony could feel that the carpeting in front of the side door wasn't too deep. He had no problem rolling over it and getting to the uncarpeted floor around their table. Tony wheeled to the table and moved the chair located on the opposite side, diagonally from where Eli was sitting, to the end of the table, opposite to where Eli's stick rested. Shoving the chair opposite to where Eli was sitting to the space vacated by the chair that was now at the end of the table, Tony wheeled in and sat across from Eli. Everything was perfect.

But the bathroom. That was a bonus. Eli thought this was especially perfect, and so did Tony. Right there, the bathroom was right there. Stand up, grab the white stick, turn around, and follow the wall on the right for three or four feet. Turn the corner to the right and follow the wall for a few feet until it came to an end. Turn left ninety degrees, walk a few more feet, and there it is—the white stick hits the opposite wall. Turn right, follow the wall for a few more feet, and—*boom*—bathroom door.

Tony had shown Eli the bathroom on their first visit to the bar. Wide door. Wheelchair in easily. Follow the wall on the right for a few feet. Turn right. When it ends, a few more steps and—*boom*—three urinals. Perfect! Turn left. Walk a few steps and—*boom*—two sinks. On the wall to the left and above the second sink—*boom*—paper towels. Perfect. Across from the sinks, two cubicles. One with a nice wide door. Roll the wheelchair in, no problem. Everything was perfect.

"Hey. Sorry, guys." The server laughed nervously as she stood at the end of their table.

"What's up?" Tony said.

"Well, sorry, but I have to see some ID."

"ID!" Eli exploded in laughter.

"But we already had a couple of beers!" Tony said.

"I know. I know. See...my manager—the manager just started his shift for the night, the night shift, and told me, 'Check the ID on those guys.'"

"The thing is," Eli said, "we already been drinking beer here, and we been here couple times before. Besides dat, the dude there"—Eli tilted his chin and pointed it toward Tony—"he probably...he probably fifty, sixty years old. He ancient."

All three of them were laughing now, though the server still laughed nervously.

"Come on," Tony said. "I mean, look at us. Do we look under twenty-one? I mean...I mean, we're pushing thirty."

"Yeah. But we bein' flattered!" Eli said.

"Yeah, yeah. But c'mon! What's goin' on?" Tony said.

"Okay, okay," the server said. "The thing is—okay, the thing is, it's, see, this manager...." The server lowered her voice. "He's just a little uptight. It's not you guys. He's just a little uptight. He's just worried, you know, liability. 'They will blame me if they don't get home all right. I'd be liable.'"

"Ohhhhh," Eli said. "Man, I get it. I get it, man. He thinks we be drunk in a while, and we, the two of us crips, can't be makin' it down the street. I get it."

Tony and Eli exaggerated their laughter now. On Tony's signal, they attempted a high-five but missed, feigning drunkenness.

"Yeahhh, man," Eli said. "Hey, Tony, we two crips. And we druuuuunk." Eli slurred his words and swiveled in his chair, keeping up the drunk act. "We get out on the street there, annnnd...who da fuck know what happen?"

"Right. And you grab onto the back of my wheelchair 'cauuuse I'm driving. I'm DUI."

"Yeah. Right, man. You in that tiiiiitanium chair, and you boogying down the street real fast and...and...I hangin' on the back. Dat's cool...dat's cool. Den I take my white stick...and...and...hop on it straight down the street. I say...I say...get out the way, mutherfuckas. D'street be ours. We got...we gots dis white crip in a wheelchair and dis black blind dude. Weee comin' down the street fast. We goin' DUI—get out d'way!"

Eli and Tony were laughing almost hysterically now. The server joined them, her laugh now more relaxed.

"Serious. Serious, man," Eli said. "We okay...we okay."

"I know. I know," the server said.

"Yeah. We're good," Tony said.

"Yeah," Eli said. "What you do is you send dat uptight manager over here. We talk to th' dude, nice and gentle. We fix it up. Don't worry."

"We'll take care of it," Tony said.

"Right. We be okay," Eli said. "Hey, Tony, let's flash our ID and get on with our business."

"Curb," Eli thought. *You can't really call it a curb.* There was no curb—a little lip, but no curb. He searched for the little lip with his white stick, moving it more gently from left to right. He didn't want to miss it and end up in the street.

Eli put everything into action at this crucial point. He touched the sidewalk with his white stick, an extension of his hand and fingers, really. He listened to the traffic flow. He heard the traffic, cars moving from left to right in front of him. He was approaching a red light, no cars moving on his left. He could sense that the light was red.

Wait! Stop! Was that the lip? No. Eli didn't think so.

They sat in the bar, Eli and Tony, drinking their beer, not speaking. They sat, taking a breather, or so it seemed. They experienced stuff like this many times. People thought all sorts of things of them.

"It must be awful being blind," they said.

"It must be awful being confined to a wheelchair, bound to it," they said.

"I couldn't live like that," they said.

"You're blind. You shouldn't be drinking," they said.

"You're confined to a wheelchair. You shouldn't be drinking," they said.

The things people said to them made Eli and Tony laugh, but it also made them sad. Sometimes they had to fight the temptation, slight as it was, to think these things of themselves. They had to remember that they were just like those people—before he lost his sight, before he was confined to a wheelchair.

But they were different now. They were no longer just like those people. They were only like them...a little. They were just like those people, but not. They were different from those people; they were something more, and, from the point of view of "those people," they were something less.

"Y'all right, bro?" Eli said, breaking the silence. "You realllll quiet."

"Yeah...you too, man."

"True dat," Eli said. "But you know what, man?"

"What?"

"It like dis, man. It like dis. We gots t'laugh."

"What! Laugh! You saying we gotta laugh?"

"Yeah, man. Yeah. Laugh! See, dem people, like dat manager, see, dey don't know shit about us. Dey only know what dey wanna know. Cut 'em off. Card 'em. Dat's just shit. You know dat's shit."

"Yeah."

"We know different. We can drink. Shit, we go to university. We gots to laugh. We gots to, y'know, we gots t'kinda humour dem. Maybe den...maybe den we change their image 'bout us."

"I know, Eli. And...and we did laugh. Remember?"

"Yeah."

"I do laugh. I do. I do. But then it comes over me. I think, 'Ah fuck. Why do I have to humour them?' How come we got to always make *them* feel comfortable around *us*? It makes me sad to know what people think about us. Strangers! People don't even know us, and they still think all this garbage about us. It makes me sad sometimes, Eli. Makes me sad."

"I know, man. Me too. But it not just to make them feel 'commmfortable.' I mean, come on. Who gives a shit if dey comfortable or not? We comfortable. And then...and then...they makes *us* uncomfortable. 'Check the ID. Dey can't be drinkin'.' Yeah, dat makes me uncomfortable, and sad too."

"See...that's what I mean. That's what I'm talking about."

"I know. I know, Tony. But...what I'm sayin'—I'm sayin' when dat shit happens, like before with dat manager.... I'm sayin'—I'm sayin' we *gots* t'laugh! If we don't, man, we cryin'. We gots to laugh just...just to keep from cryin'."

"You're right. You're right. I know, but sometimes, Eli...."

"Yeah. Yeah, I know, Tony. I'm like you. I'm sad—sad and sometimes I'm cryin'. But...but I'm usually *pissed*. I be *pissed*. Laughin' keep me from cryin', and laughin' keep me from being more pissed."

"I know," Tony said. "What do people know? They don't even know us. I mean, we're—you and me—we're going to fuckin' university! We didn't even dream of going to university before this shit happened to us. People don't know that."

"You sayin'—you sayin' this crip shit that happened to us *made* us go to university? You sayin' this blind thing and this rolling-stock thing is good?"

"Well, we're in university, aren't we? That's a good thing, isn't it?"

"Could be. Maybe. But what else do I do? Get a trade? Trade," Eli said, now laughing. "I see it now. Make way! Make way for the blind plumber! He comin' t'fix your toilet!"

Tony joined Eli in his laughter. They were both laughing almost scornfully now at the way others regarded them.

"Or, or, or, make way! Here come the blind

welder! See, he got those protective goggles! No way his eyes get hurt. No way he go blind *again!*"

"Yeah, man. Yeah. Okay, okay! Here comes that rolling-stock cop! Stop running, criminals! *Rollo*Cop is gonna run you down! Spread 'em, muthafucka!"

Eli and Tony were laughing uncontrollably. Eli's hand was pounding the table, and Tony's hand was banging the arm of his wheelchair. In a few moments, their laughter subsided, then it became sporadic gasps as if they had been holding their breath.

"Oh, man," Eli said, taking his dark glasses off and rubbing his eyes. "Oh, man. Dat's funny shit, man."

"Fuck. That's real funny," Tony said. "Hey, Eli.... Cheers, man."

Eli held his pint of beer at his chest, slightly in front of him. Tony held up his pint of beer and moved it toward Eli's.

Clink.

There were several people at the corner, given all the voices he was hearing.

"Hello. Hello." The greeting came to Eli loudly and cheerfully. Was it someone he knew? That was possible. They didn't say his name though. Could be someone he knew. Those sighties—they thought that all blind people had super hearing. *Just say hello. Don't tell him who you are. He'll rec-*

ognize you. He's got super hearing.

Better say hello in case I know her.

"Hi," Eli said as loudly and as cheerfully as she had.

"I'm a little late. Sorry! No, no, I'm only, like, five minutes away. See you soon. Right. Bye."

Fucking cellphone, Eli thought. He hated when people used them on the street. *"Talking to me?" "Nah, I'm on the phone."*

He took a couple of steps back. He didn't know why he did this. He just did it.

"Oh, sorry," the man behind him said as Eli bumped into him.

"No, no. That's me. Sorry," Eli said.

Sudden movements, sudden and quick steps back, to the left, to the right. Cellphones, bumping into people. He was disoriented.

Eli stood still. He needed to get reoriented. He listened to the traffic flow, letting it tell him whether he was facing the street he wanted to cross, whether he was facing the intersecting street, whether he was facing it at an angle....

"Hey, how y'all doin'?" the man said, leaning on the chair at the end of the table.

"Good. We're good," Eli and Tony said.

"Listen. Sorry. I'm sorry, y'all."

Eli and Tony were looking at him quizzically, wondering who he was and what he was sorry for.

"I'm, uh...I'm, uh, Justin. I'm the manager."

"Ahhh," Tony said. "You're the maaanager. You're the one that needs to see our ID."

"Yeah. Yeah, I'm the one. Sorry. You...you...." The manager held his hand out toward Tony. "You. What's your name?"

"I'm Tony." He held his hand out to the manager. "Tony, aaand you're Justin, right?"

"Yeah, man. Good. Good t'meet ya, Tony."

"Good to meet you too."

"And you, my brother. What's your name?"

Eli quickly extended his hand to the manager. He always did this when meeting someone for the first time. *Better have my hand out first*, Eli reasoned, *then they'll shake it. Beats me groping for their hand.* "Eli. Eli, man. Good to meet you, Justin."

The two shook hands. Justin had a firm hand. This made Eli strengthen his own handshake. Eli wondered why he did this. It wasn't as though he was competing with Justin in some handshaking contest. And yet Eli felt he had to return the familiarity of the greeting.

"Soooo," Eli said, "you the one who give the waitress, uhhh, what's her name?"

"Sally," Justin said. "Sally."

"Sally," Eli continued. "All right, you the one who tells Sally to check us out. You say, 'Sally, go check those two. See how old they are.'" Tony was laughing a little. "You say, 'Card 'em.'"

"Yeahhh," Justin said slowly. "Yeah, I—look, oh, sorry. See, ah, all right. Yeah, I messed up. Sorry."

"But..." Tony said, "but you don't think Eli and me is too young to be drinkin', do you?"

"Nah, nah, nah. You two all right."

"Then," Tony continued, "why did you tell, uh...Sally. Sally. Why did you tell her to ID us?"

"Yeah, man," Eli said, taking over from Tony. "You came in after we was already here. Dat's what Sally said. So you *seen*...." Eli and Tony laughed. Justin did, too, but just a little. "You *seen* Tony and me weren't no spring chickens," Eli continued.

"That's right," Tony resumed. "You saw us. No need for ID."

"I know. I know. You two are right. You know, honestly...honestly...okay—I messed up. I messed up!"

"Right, man. You walk in the door back there," Eli said, jerking his thumb to the rear. "You den see nobody sittin' up here in th'front. You don't even see us two. You see the white stick standin' up here and you see the wheelchair. You don't see us, just the stick and the chair. And then you be thinking—"

"I know. You're right, brother. I freaked out some. I'm thinkin', 'Oh, shit, I got a blind brother and I got a dude in a wheelchair. Shit.' I'm thinkin', 'I don't want those two drinkin' and drinkin' and leavin' my bar—and havin' some kinda accident. It's not right, but that's what I'm thinkin'.'"

"Okay," Tony said. "At least you're honest.

Gotta appreciate that."

Tony held his fist out to Justin for a fist bump.

"There," Tony said.

"We cool?" Justin said.

"Hey, Eli. Fist bump," Tony said.

"We cool, bro," Justin said, holding his fist out to Eli.

"We cool, man," Eli said.

Eli held his fist out to Justin. *Bonk.* Eli smiled. He knew—he was pretty sure—that Justin's fist was already facing him, and he was happy that there was no groping. Just *fist-bumping.*

The three of them laughed and exchanged some pleasantries.

"It's a great bar," Eli and Tony told Justin.

Justin told them that he had been working there for about six years, the last two as night manager.

"Okay, guys," he said then. "Okay, uh...Eli, Tony, right?"

Eli and Tony smiled and nodded.

"The next two beers is on the house," said Justin.

"No need," Eli said. "No need, but thanks for the free booze. 'Preciate it."

"No prob. My pleasure." Justin turned and began making his way to the bar.

"Hopes we don't get drunk and get kill't on the way home," Eli said, laughing at the retreating Justin.

"Man," Eli said, turning his body to face Tony.

"Yeah, no shit. He's gone now, Eli."

"Hey, Tony."

"Yeah?"

"That man a brother, Tony?"

"Yeah."

"Okay, gentlemen," Justin said as he returned to the table a few minutes later. "Two beers, on the house!"

"Hey, Tony, now we 'gentlemens.'"

The three of them laughed.

"There you go, Tony," Justin said. "Aaand yours, my brother. Okay, I'm takin' your empty and putting your full one right exactly where the empty was."

"Thank you, my brother."

"Thanks," Tony said.

"Enjoy. You guys are good." And with that, Justin retreated once again.

"What were you sayin', Eli? Oh, clear, he's gone. Before he brought us our beer?"

"No, no. Nuthin'. I was just thinkin'. Remember that course we took together, that SOC101 course? 'Member it had all those names? There be, like, *genderrr, classs, raaace*. Y'know, all that shit."

"Yeah, I remember. But remember—there was nooo 'disability' on that list. Remember?"

"I *do*, man. But, Tony, 'member what *you* said to the prof?"

They both laughed and then sipped their beer.

"You said—you said, '*Excuse me.*' I love how you say 'excuse me.' And *then* you put your hand up. What's that about?"

"I dunno," Tony said, still laughing.

"Anyway, anyway, you say, "Scuuuuse me. How come disability ain't on that list?' Remember?"

"I didn't say 'ain't.'" Tony laughed.

"Ah, shaddup."

They fell into a comfortable silence. As they sat embracing it, they knew that they liked this bar. Eli thought of Sally, the waitress. She wasn't a rolling stocker, Eli knew, and she certainly wasn't blind. He wondered, though, if she was pretty.

Great! The 'L' train is leaving the station. The light's red for them but green for me.

It's green! Got the blend, got the street, it's green! Go!

The dull sound that came after screeching tires and blaring horns wasn't as loud as it was sickening.

Eli landed with a thud. He knew that he was down, and he knew that he shouldn't have stepped off the blended curb so quickly. No pain. He couldn't feel any, anyway. Eli wondered what had happened. *How come I'm down?* Lots of lights. *Man, this is weird. Never saw no lights for years. Lots of them now though. Can't really move. No point trying. Not sure how to move. Gotta get up though. Yeah, gotta get up...but it's kinda nice down here....*

"ELIIIIIIII!"

Tony's calling me. Oh, I think I remember. Tony's telling me to get out of the way. Maybe I'll just stay down here a little bit, get rested, Eli thought.

And then...all was darkness.

Chasing Sight[1]

She's beautiful! He was surprised at just how beautiful she was. And then he felt guilty. Immediately. Why was he surprised? Well, she *was* beautiful after all. But, still, he felt guilty.

He was looking at her, staring really. And he felt guilty about this too. He was looking at her, noticing how beautiful she was. *Why am I looking at her—in that way?* he asked himself. *I shouldn't be doing this. This is ridiculous.*

He jerked his eyes from Jenny, and this surprised him even more than the fact that he was looking at her while realizing how beautiful she was. He tried to return his eyes to her but, to his surprise, discovered that he couldn't. That made him feel even more ridiculous. *It doesn't matter whether I look at her or not*, he thought. *What's my problem?*

"You okay, Phil?" Jenny said.

"Oh, yeah. Yeah. Yeah, I'm good. Good."

"It's just, you know—I'm just...I noticed you were kinda quiet."

"Right. No. It's this, uh, it's this reading aloud.

[1] With excerpts from H.G. Wells's short story "The Country of the Blind" (1904).

Guess I'm not used to it. My throat's kinda dry."

"Oh," Jenny said. "You wanna take a break or something?"

"No," Phil said. "I think I'll be fine. I got some. I need some—just a little. I'll just drink a little water, and I'll be okay."

"You sure?"

"Yeah. You know, dry throat, from reading aloud."

"Sorry...."

"No, no, no. Don't be sorry. It's not your—"

"I know," Jenny interrupted. "But you've been going for, like, let's see...." She touched the watch on her left wrist. She flipped the tiny lid open and felt its face. "Let's see. Yeah, you've been reading for just over half an hour."

"A little water, and I'll be fine," Phil said.

"This is your first time doing this, isn't it?" Jenny said.

"Yeah."

"Well. Well, we're here for two hours, and we got about an hour and a half left. By that time, you won't be able to talk at all." Jenny laughed. "Here's what we should do. Read for half an hour, take a break. Read for half an hour, take a break. Like that."

"Okay," Phil said, laughing. "Okay, you know best."

"I sure do."

"All right, then," Phil said. "What about a coffee? Do you—?"

"That's great! Is there somewhere close?"

"Yeah. Just at the end of the hall. There's, uhhh, I think it's a Second Cup."

They were seated across from one another at a table in the coffee shop, their hands wrapped around cups of coffee.

I can't believe I'm so fucking stupid, Phil thought. *I took her hand! I took her hand! I can't believe I did that.*

Phil was very embarrassed. He knew better than to take Jenny's hand. Guiding blind people was something he learned weeks ago at the training session for volunteers. They showed him, he was thinking now. *They showed me, showed me, showed me....* They showed him how to guide a blind person. *First chance I get*, Phil thought, *I blow it. I—take—her—hand. Shit!*

"You can guide me to the coffee shop, right?" Jenny had said to him as they were leaving the reading room and heading to Second Cup.

"Oh, yes," Phil had said confidently. "Oh, yes, I can."

Turns out, he thought, *turns out I can't. I—took—her—hand!*

Jenny was quick though. She was quick to tell him it would be better if she took his elbow. But first, she gave Phil's hand a little squeeze and smiled. It was at that moment that the red stain of embarrassment began creeping down his face and neck. His whole body shuddered as he dropped her hand. *Did she squeeze my hand? Am I imagining things?*

"Right! Oh, right! Sorry!" Phil had said.

"It's just that, well, it's just that I can—holding your elbow this way—I can walk slightly behind you; I can follow which way you're going, follow your body—left, right, whatever."

"Yeah. Yeah, I know. Okay, here's my elbow." Phil lightly touched Jenny's left arm with his right.

I can't believe I took her hand, Phil thought as he sipped his coffee. He looked at Jenny and once more marvelled at her beauty. *Long, dark—well, darkish—hair*, he thought, looking at her. *Brown? No, it's got some red in it. What's that called? What's that called? Auburn! That's it*, he thought. *She squeezed my hand! I'm sure she did.*

He was now looking into Jenny's eyes. He marvelled at how big they were. *Wow*, he thought, *her eyes—they're...they're beautiful....*

He snapped his eyes away from her. *What the fuck am I doing?* he thought. Phil didn't know what to make of what he was doing. He knew that he was looking at Jenny and admiring her. And he knew that he felt embarrassed and even ashamed for doing so. He didn't know why he felt this. He just did.

Phil took a deep breath and eased his eyes downward to face his coffee cup.

"Man," Jenny said, "I'm, like—I'm, like, sooo totally glad we're finished with that psych article. Oh my God, that stuff's boring. But it only took half an hour, and that's totally good."

"You don't like psych?" Phil said, remembering to keep his eyes on his coffee cup.

"I dunno. I dunno. It's just, like—it's just...it makes no sense sometimes."

"Really?"

"Ummm. It's, like, well, like, it's all the brain this term. 'The brain does this.' 'The brain does that.' Like we do nothing, right? The brain does everything. We do nothing. It's like perception. We took perception. So the guy says, the prof says, eighty-five percent of what we know—I mean, of everything we know!—eighty-five percent is eyes, comes from eyesight!"

"Mm-hmm."

"Yeah. So me—me, like, if that's true, I'm eighty-five cents short of a loonie." Jenny laughed and then sipped her coffee.

Phil laughed a moment later as though Jenny's laughter gave him permission. He was looking right into her eyes! He jerked his eyes down to his coffee. He spilled a little.

"Oh, shit!"

"What!" Jenny said. "What! What happened? You okay?"

"Yeah. I'm okay. I just spilled a little coffee."

"Want a napkin?" Jenny said, laughing.

"No. No. Got one. What's so funny?"

"It's just..." Jenny began, laughing more exuberantly. "It's just, like, us blinks do that, not you sighties."

"Sighties? What's that?" Phil said.

"Yeah, sighties. That's what we call you people. You people. You know, you people who see. We call you sighties."

"That's funny," Phil said, not looking at her.

"We're always knocking stuff over. That's what sighties think. They think we blinks just knock stuff over. We just do."

"Yeah. Well, I did this time, not you."

"That's what I mean," Jenny said. "Sighties knock their coffee over, you know, spill it, and nothing. Well, we laugh, but nothing bad. But...*we* spill our coffee and it's 'Ohhh myyy Goddd, *poor* blind person. She must be *so* embarrassed. Ohhh, we feel sooo sorry for her.' You know what I mean?"

"Yeah. I get it," Phil said. Forgetting, her looked at her again. *She's so beautiful when she laughs*, he thought. *Even her eyes look like they're laughing. Her eyes are so expressive.* He really wanted to talk to her about it but knew he couldn't.

"Let's see. What time?" Jenny felt the face of her watch. "Guess it's time."

"Yup," Phil said. "Time to get back at it."

"Your throat okay?"

"Yeah. I'm good."

"At least that psych article is done," Jenny said. "The next one...the next one—I can hardly wait to read it...well, for you to read it to me."

"Yeah? What's the article?"

"Actually, it's not an article. It's, uh, it's a short story. H.G. Wells, I think the prof said. And listen." Jenny leaned slightly forward. "Listen to this. The story's called 'Country of the Blind.' Isn't that cool?"

Phil was very pleased with himself. He remembered this time. *Don't take her hand.* And yet he wondered about that squeeze from before.

"All right," Phil said as they returned to their chairs in the reading room. "Let's check it out. Well, Jenny, it's not too long. Sure looks interesting, though."

"Does it?"

"Yeah," Phil said. "Okay." He cleared his throat. "Okay, here we go." He began reading:

"*Three hundred miles and more from Ch...Kuh...Chim—boraza....*"

"What? Chim—boh—what? Spell it, okay, Phil?"

"*C—H—I—M—B—O—R—A—Z—O...one hundred from the snows of Kuh—tah—pock—see—*...I'll spell that."

"Good."

"*C—O—T—O—P—A—X—I...in the wildest wastes of Ecuador's Andes, there lies that mysterious mountain valley, cut off from the world of men—*" he took a deep breath and continued "*—the...the Country of the Blind. Long years ago that* *valley lay so far open to the world that men might come at last through frightful gorges and over an icy pass into its...ecua...ecua*—bowl? Don't know."

"What's that word?" Jenny said.

"I dunno. I'll spell it."

"*E—Q—U—A—B—L—E...that equable,* I mean, *its equable meadows; and thither indeed man came, a family or so of...Peruvian half-breeds fleeing from the lust and tyranny*—"

"Lust and tyranny?" Jenny said.

"Yeah, funny, eh? *...from the lust and tyranny of an evil Spanish ruler. Then came the stupendous outbreak of...Meen...uh...Min—dob—bamba?* I'll spell. *M—I—N—D—O—B—A—M— B—A...when it was night in Quito...Q—U—I—T—O...night in Quito for seventeen days....*"

"It's weird," Jenny said. "Must be some kind of illness or something."

"Yeah, I think so. Must be."

"Well, I guess—I guess, like, I guess he has to get a bunch of people blind somehow, you know, if they're gonna, like, have their own country."

"Right. Let's see," Phil said. "Illness, maybe. *And amidst the little population of that now isolated and forgotten valley the disease ran its course.* You're right. The disease. *The old became groping and purblind, the young saw but dimly, and children that were born to them saw never at all.*"

"That's really clever," Jenny said, interrupting Phil's reading.

"Clever?"

"Yeah. I think so," she continued. "I mean, 'Country of the Blind.' You know, it's a country, like, it needs a population, you know, like any other country."

Oh, right, I see... Phil thought but didn't say aloud. "You're right. Wells—he needs to create...to create a population, like you said. He needs a country made up of all blind people."

"Yeah, so what better way to get a whole bunch of blinks than to create some kind of disease? What better way? I suppose. And then...and then...did you notice? He made them blind over generations. At first, when the disease hit, they could see a little. What did he call it? Oh, yeah, 'dimly'...."

"Right," Phil said. "Hey, Jenny?"

"Yeah?"

"Can I ask you a question before we start reading again?"

"Sure."

"What's this, Jenny? What's this 'blink' thing? I'm a 'sightie' and you're a 'blink'? Is that right?"

"See...."

Phil began smiling. To his surprise, his embarrassment was waning.

"See," Jenny continued, "I'm a blink. I'm a citizen in the Country of the Blinks."

"I get it. You're funny, Jenny."

"Well," Jenny said, "you gotta laugh at this

stuff, don't you? At least sometimes."

"I guess so. But so far, this story doesn't have any humour in it. You know what I mean? And you're right. Wells had to create a whole country of blind people. And he had to make them blind, you know, like from the children, and so he made them, these blind people, I mean, these 'blinks.'" Phil laughed. "He made it, you know, with this disease so that the children, and then they grew up, like, they had no idea what it was *not* to be blind."

"That's right," Jenny said. "They had no idea of what it meant to see. They didn't know what sight was. You know, that's cool. I think that's cool."

A silence then crept in between them. Phil wondered what it was like not to know what sight meant and not to know what it meant to see. He wondered if Jenny knew.

"This stuff, this English stuff, is *way* better than psych," Jenny said.

"Well? Keep going?" Phil said.

"Yeah."

Phil began coughing after another ten minutes of reading.

"You okay?"

"Yeah. Yeah," Phil said. "I just need a little water. There, that's good."

"I hope..." Jenny said, "I hope he's going to— what's his name? Nunez?—I hope he's going to find out soon whether these people are blind or not. I mean, I know they are. But I'm looking forward to how he's gonna *deal* with them—you know, how he's going to *talk* to them."

"That'll be interesting, yeah," Phil said. "Oh! Here it is, right here. It's coming up next."

"Great!"

Phil read: "*When at last, after much shouting and wrath, Nunez crossed the stream by a little bridge, came through a gate in the wall, and approached them, he was sure that they were blind. He was sure that this was the Country of the Blind of which the legends told. Conviction had sprung upon him, and a sense of great and rather enviable adventure.*"

"Finally!" Jenny said. "Finally! The sightie's convinced! That Nunez...all those other signs he saw—the houses painted all in funny ways, arranged in really straight lines —all that stuff didn't convince him. Even when he waved at them and they didn't wave back, you know? He's not convinced 'til he's right up to them, right up to them blind people."

"Yeah. Yeah, that's true."

"It's like you sighties—well, I don't mean you, Phil; I mean Nunez—it's like he doesn't know anything unless he can see it! You know, he comes right up to them. Who knows? Maybe...maybe he looks in their eyes and their eyes aren't moving. Then he sees they're blind."

"Yeah, Jenny."

Phil was feeling less embarrassed minute by minute. This was still surprising, though, and, again, he didn't know why.

"You're right," he continued. "It's sort of, like, well, it's like *we sighties*"—he laughed at this—"we have to be convinced of things. We have to *see it*." Once more he was surprised at his lack of embarrassment. "It's weird. But I think you've got something there, Jenny."

"You know, Phil, you're right. There's something there. Like, it's like the knowledge thing. It's, like, well, it's like, you know eighty-five percent more than I do. That's funny, eh? According to psych, and probably according to Nunez too, I only know a little of what you know."

"Yeah." Phil's embarrassment returned and this time with bells on.

"Do you think all sighties think that about us blinks? You don't think that, do you? I don't think you think that."

Phil looked into Jenny's eyes once more. *She's looking at me*, he thought. *Right at me. She can't see me, but she's looking at me. It's like she can see me.* He fidgeted in his chair. He was not convinced that she couldn't see him. *Maybe*, he thought, *not physically, but she can see me.*

"No, Jenny. I think you know a lot."

"Oh, you do, do you?"

"Yeah."

"I believe you. I can't see you, but I believe you."

"You know, Jenny. I was thi— I mean, I was wo— I mean..."

"What?"

"You know— No, nothing."

"Well, it's gotta be something," Jenny said.

"You know what? Let's keep reading, and I'll tell you what I was thinking at our next coffee break. Okay?"

"Okay."

He began reading: "'*Over the mountains I come,' said Nunez, 'out of a country beyond there—where men can see. From near Bogota, where there are a hundred thousands of people, and where the city passes out of sight.'*

"'*Sight?' uttered Pedro. 'Sight?'*

"'*He comes,' said the second blind man, 'out of the rocks.'*"

Jenny sat up straight. Her eyes were fixed, it seemed, on some point directly in front of her; it appeared as though she was looking directly at Phil as he sat there reading aloud. She closed her eyes and listened intently.

After ten minutes or so had passed, she interrupted his reading.

"Uh, Phil, sorry."

"Yeah?"

"Sorry to stop—I mean, sorry to interrupt you," Jenny said.

"No, no. It's cool. I need some, uh, water anyway. It's dry in here—my throat."

"Okay. Good," she said. "I was just thinking, you know. It was a few pages back—maybe two, three, I don't know. I heard you turning pages, but

I lost count, so I don't know how far back it was. But remember Nunez was telling those blind guys where he came from?"

"Yeah," Phil said as he began flipping pages, looking back in the text.

"It was where...where he said—Nunez—he said he came from where there were hundreds of thousands of people and then something about 'the city passes out of sight,' something like that. And—"

"Oh! Right!" Phil said. "Yeah, here it is. Okay, okay. He says near Bogota, yeah, here: *where the city passes out of sight.*"

"That's it! That's it. And then see where, uh, whatsisname—Pedro! Pedro! Yeah, Pedro—"

"Great memory, Jenny."

"Yeah, that's us blinks for you. Anyway, Pedro says something like, 'Sight? Sight?' See that?"

"Yeah. Right here. It says...it says 'muttered.' It says Pedro muttered 'sight' twice."

"I know! Twice! I think, you know, like, it's really cool."

"What is?"

"Well, it's just that Pedro—like, he's never seen his whole life, and Nunez uses the word *sight*, something perfectly normal, and Pedro gets bent out of shape and says, 'What is that? Sight?' And you know what else is funny?"

"What?"

"Well, just before Nunez says the word *sight*, before that he says the word *see*. But Pedro doesn't say, 'See? What's that?' He just says, 'Sight?'"

"Man, Jenny—"

"It just seems to me.... It seems to me that if you—I don't mean *you*; I mean anyone...."

"I know."

"Like, if you don't know something, I mean *really* don't know something, then, well, you just can't recognize it. It's like someone says a word you haven't even heard of and you don't have a clue. Like, if someone shows you something, like, puts it in your hands, and you don't know this thing, well, you wouldn't know what it is. Okay, you might know it's made out of wood, metal, or whatever, but you wouldn't know what it is. You couldn't *name* it."

"Yeah...."

"Yeah, so Pedro heard the words. He knew Nunez was speaking. Pedro knew what talking was. So he heard the word *see* and then the word *sight*, and then he stops Nunez and says, 'What? Sight?' He first hears the word *see* but lets it go. He figures, *Well, I'll get what that means when this guy, Nunez, talks some more.* But right after he says the word *see*, Nunez hits Pedro with *sight*! So now Pedro says, 'Sight?' He thinks, *What the fuck? What's sight?* See what I mean?"

Phil almost came out of his chair. His right hand dropped the pages he was reading and leapt to his open mouth, covering it.

Jesus Christ! he thought but didn't say. *Jesus, she's swearing! She's looking right at me. And swearing! She must be, what, twenty, and she's blind, she's fucking blind! She's beautiful and swearing. What the hell is my problem? Her hands! Her hands are flying everywhere. Shit! She's gonna knock her fucking water all over the place! I gotta move that water outta the way.*

Phil started to come out of his chair and then suddenly sat back down again. The redness of embarrassment spread over his face once more, and this time it commingled with the colour of anxiety.

No! he thought. *No! She won't know. She won't see me. When I tell her I moved her water.... Christ, that might really embarrass her.*

Jenny continued to speak enthusiastically and with great animation. "See what I mean? It's just that no one questions sight. I've never heard it questioned before. I don't even question it! In my psych course—in my psych course, they just talk about how sight works, all the neurons, stuff like that. But no one ever says, 'Sight? What the fuck is that?'"

Phil could see Jenny's hand, her right hand, moving back and forth quickly and dangerously close to her glass of water. He was very distracted by this, and he didn't hear anything she was saying. *Better do something, man*, he said to himself.

"Jenny! Jenny! Whoa! Easy."

"What? What's up?"

"Your hand, your right hand—you're gonna knock your water over."

"Oh, shit! Thanks."

She wasn't upset, angry, anything. *She said thanks. She actually said thanks.* This surprised him.

"Your hands were flying all over the place. I thought for sure that water was going to go everywhere."

"Wow," Jenny said. "Someone else told me I talk with my hands when I get excited. That's just not a cool thing for blinks to do. I'll tell you that."

"No. It's all right," Phil said.

"I know. But you wanna know a secret?"

"Yeah."

"Okay. But this is a secret, so don't tell."

"No, no. Not a soul. I won't tell a soul."

"Okay. If you promise."

"Promise."

"'Caaause this is embarrassing. I've knocked stuff over before with my hands."

"Really!"

"Yeah, really. Okay, here's the secret. One time, I was meeting one of my profs in her office. She was real nice. She said, 'Hey, Jenny.' She showed me her chair, the desk, where to sit, all like that. Then she says, 'Want a coffee? I'm getting one for myself.' So I figure, what the fuck, sure I'll have a coffee. So she goes out and then comes back with two coffees. She was real nice. She said, 'Okay, Jenny, here's your coffee, right in front of you.' And—this is the great thing—she knew, she actually knew, to hold onto the coffee 'cause it was one of those—one of those paper cups? Like the one from before we had in the coffee shop?"

"Yeah."

"So it's all good. I find the coffee, wrap my hand around it, so everything's cool. So then she says, 'Uh, so, Jenny, you wanna talk about your paper, right?' 'Yes I do,' I told her. 'I want to talk about my paper.' By the way, I kind of like my paper, or at least the idea I was having to write it."

"What was it? What sort of idea?"

"Oh. Oh, right. Okay, in my Canadian lit class? We had to write a ten-page paper on a theme from a novel—you know, one of the novels we read in class. So I pick *The Meeting Place*—uh, no, no, *The Meeting Point*. Yeah that's it. *Point*. It's by, uh, Clarke! Yeah, Austin Clarke."

"Never read it. Is it good?"

"It's awesome! These people from Barbados—well, the women. I was interested most in the women from Barbados. Anyway, they move to Toronto. But they're all 'domestics'—that's what they called them in that time. 'Domestics.' You know, they clean people's houses—rich people...well, rich white people. They clean their houses and all that shit."

"Mm-hmm."

"So...so in class? They're all talking about how much we learned about Barbados—you know, Barbadian culture—from the book. And, okay, we do. But then it hits me! This book is about Toronto! Well, Barbados too. But mostly Toronto! It's about Toronto in the fifties and sixties, I think.

It's about Toronto! White Toronto! White fucking racist Toronto! So, I figure, this is great! But I think I better check it with the prof. That's why I went to see her."

"Okay."

"So anyway, I'm in her office. I've got my coffee in my hand. It's on the desk. I know where it is. Everything's cool, right?"

"Right."

"Nooo! Wrong! I start telling the prof about my paper. She gets excited. She actually gets excited! So I get excited. So you know what happened. You saw it. I get excited; I talk with my hands. *Boom!* There goes the fucking coffee. All—over—her—desk! She jumps up; I jump up. I'm saying *sorry sorrysorrysorry*; she's saying *itsokayitsokay*. I was *so—fucking—embarrassed*. So there's my secret. Don't tell a soul."

Phil was laughing. He was not feeling embarrassed at all. "That's amazing!" he said. "But everything turned out okay, did it?"

"Oh, yeah. Yeah. Yeah. No, I've been to her office lots of times after that. And now it's cool 'cause, well, like, we have this joke. Like, I come in, find the chair, sit. Then she says, each time, 'Hey, Jenny, *want a coffee?*'"

"That's funny."

"Yeah. She's so cool. And, by the way, she really liked my idea for that paper. Aaactually...." Jenny began moving her hand toward Phil. "I wonder. There just might be something in this

H.G. Wells story that I might be able to use in that other paper."

"Whoa, Jenny. Your hand." Phil put his hand on Jenny's. "You're gonna knock your water over."

"Oh, fuck. Thanks."

Fuck, Phil thought. *She's squeezing my hand! For sure! This time for sure!*

"Hey, Phil," she said, slowly letting go of his hand, "is there much to go in this story?"

"What!" He could barely make out what she was saying.

"How much is left in the story?"

"Oh. I'd say, uh, ten minutes? Maybe fifteen at the most."

"You wanna finish it and go for a coffee?" She laughed. "Coffee? Get it?"

"Yeah. Let's finish and go for a coffee. I'd like that." Phil laughed a little.

"Cool."

Phil began reading. Jenny listened even more intently than before.

"'Why did you not come when I called you?' said the blind man. 'Must you be led like a child? Cannot you hear the path as you walk?'"

Phil's eyebrows rose slightly.

"Nunez laughed. 'I can see it,' he said.

"'There is no such word as see,' said the blind man, after a pause. 'Cease this folly, and follow the sound of my feet.'"

They sat across from each other. This time, though, they were at a café, Bar Mercurio on Bloor Street. It was quiet in the café, with only a few other people occupying a couple of tables.

Three o'clock, Thursday afternoon, Phil thought, *relatively quiet, peaceful even.*

"Nice comfy chairs," Jenny said. She extended her hands, slowly and carefully, touching both ends of the table.

A server approached them. "What can I get for you?" she asked Phil.

"Uhhh, I think—I think I'll have a latte. Yeah. Latte. Skim milk, if you have it."

"Skim milk it is," the server said cheerfully. She then looked at Jenny, said nothing, and slowly cast her look back to Phil.

The server had a quizzical look on her face, Phil noticed. *Why is she looking at me? I already told her what I wanted.*

"And what about her?" the server said. "What's she gonna have?"

Jenny straightened. Her right hand tightened on the edge of the table. Her eyes closed a little. She wasn't smiling anymore.

Phil wasn't sure what to do, and embarrassment began to creep up his face. He looked at the server and opened his mouth and then quickly shut it. He looked at Jenny. She sat there, straight as a rod, with a blank expression on her face. No smile, no big eyes—they were gone.

Phil then noticed that, very slowly, a smile

started to make its way onto Jenny's lips. Her eyes opened wide, he saw. It seemed as though she flicked them at the server. She flicked her eyes. Phil saw her do it. *She actually flicked them!* he thought.

Phil suddenly felt tense. It was the feeling of waiting, anticipating, of not knowing what was coming next. His left hand gripped the edge of the table tightly. He was watching Jenny.

To his surprise, Jenny's eyes moved from the server and rested upon his face, and she spoke, very slowly. *"What will I have, Phil?"*

Everything seemed to happen all at once. Phil's hand leapt to his open mouth, covering it. Almost simultaneously, the server's hand sprung to Phil's shoulder, gripping it tightly. They were looking, wide-eyed, at each other. Jenny's posture had relaxed. She was smiling. She turned her face slowly to the right and fixed her gaze at a point just to the right and above Phil's shoulder. All of this happened so quickly.

"Oh my God!" the server said.

"She *can!*" Phil said.

"I'm sor—so sor—!" the server stammered.

"Ask! Ask h—!" Phil said.

"Oh my God!" the server said again.

"She can!" Phil said again.

Jenny released her grip on the table. She then seemed to enjoy this clear display of embarrassment. She began to laugh. "You two guys havin' fun? Don't mean to interrupt your good times, but

I need to order a coffee."

The server jerked her eyes from Phil to Jenny. Her hand dropped from Phil's shoulder. Her other hand leapt to Jenny's shoulder. As she did this, she spoke to her, almost hysterically, "I'm so sor—"

Jenny's body bounced, startled by the sudden touch on her shoulder.

"Oh my God!" the server said. "Oh my God! I did it again! I'm sorry." She snapped her hand back.

"Easy. It's cool," Jenny said, still laughing.

Phil watched all of this. He sat straight up in his chair, red-faced, his hand transferred from his mouth to the edge of the table. He sat immobile, gripping both edges of the table.

"Think I can order now?" Jenny said, mustering up as much ironic sweetness as she could.

"Yes! Yes! I'm sooo sorry!" the server said.

"Great. I'll have an Americano, milk and sugar please."

"Americano! Absolutely! Absolutely! Milk and sugar! Americano!"

"Thanks."

The server turned and began to walk away quickly. Just as quickly, she turned and jogged back to Jenny. She put her hand on her shoulder again and said, "Sorry! Sorry! Be right back! I'm leaving!"

"It's okay," Jenny said, patting the server's hand in the most condescending way she could muster.

"Be right back! Americano, milk and sugar!" And she was off and running.

Jenny was still laughing as she turned toward Phil, who, although more relaxed now, was still red-faced. In what seemed like a second, the server was back.

"I forgot! I forgot! Oh my God, I forgot! What are you going to—"

"He'll—have—a latte," Jenny said.

The server stood still, looking at Jenny. Suddenly, a look of awareness came across her face. "Latte. Right. Be right back," she said.

Jenny was silent. Phil looked at her. *What the fuck just happened?* he wondered.

"Good coffee, eh?" Phil said.

"Mmm, mmm. Well, one thing's for sure; they sure know how to make Americanos here."

"Yours is good too, huh?" Phil said.

"Mm-hmm! Sure is."

They sat in silence, drinking their coffee. Phil was looking at Jenny. She was looking at him, or so it seemed. He found this disconcerting.

"You know what?" Jenny said, breaking the silence.

"What?"

"You know what would be funny?"

"What?"

"Well, say, like, uh, like, say the next time we're here...."

Next time! Next time! Phil thought. *Did I hear right? That's what she said! "Next time"! "Next time* we're *here"! She didn't say, "Next time* I'm *here." She said, "Next time* we're *here"!* Phil heard Jenny's voice. She was still speaking, but his mind was elsewhere. He was looking at her hands.

"Sorry. Pardon?" he said.

"Were you somewhere else there?" Jenny said.

"Yeah—no. I was just thinkin' about...about what happened. It was weird."

"Yeah. But it would be really funny—really funny—if, like, the next time we're here aaand she says to me, 'What will you have?' I should say—this would be funny—I should say, like, 'I don't know. Ask him what I want.' Wouldn't that be hilarious?"

"Oh my God! That would be *so* funny. Totally," Phil said.

"Hey, Phil?"

"Yeah?"

"What if, like, what if I stumbled out of the chute—you know, being born...?"

"Yeah," Phil said, laughing.

"No. Seriously. Serious. What if, when I was born, like, *blind*...? Like, I'm born blind and I stumble into the—get this!—I stumble into the *Country of the Sighted.*"

"Oh, I get it."

"Yeah!" Jenny said. She lowered her hands to the table. She found her coffee cup, held it with one hand, and played with the coffee spoon with the other. She looked at the coffee cup and then at Phil. "A country," Jenny said. "I mean, an actual country! That is sooo totally different—like, it's one thing to be in the Country of the Sighted, and it's a whole different deal, I mean, to have your own country! I mean a *country* of the blind!" She fell silent once more.

"You know," Phil said, breaking the silence, "they showed us this report a couple of weeks ago—I mean, the people who trained us to do this reading aloud stuff. I think it was by the World Health Organization. They said—get this—they said there were about a billion disabled people around the world. A billion!"

"Really?"

"Yeah. A *billion.*"

"Wow! A billion of us! We could have our own country—the *Country of the Disabled.* That would be cool."

"Yeah."

"I mean, a billion—that's a big country. Way bigger than Canada. And you know what else is funny? Well, we could have our own country, and with a billion of us, we could have our own military. Isn't that a hoot?"

They both laughed and drank their coffee. Jenny looked at her coffee cup. She became serious. "Actually," she said. "I was thinking, actually. I was thinking about what that blind guy said to Nunez."

"Which part? When?"

"It was, uh, when the blind guy asked Nunez why he didn't come when he called him. Remember?"

"Sort of."

"Well, anyway, he said—he said to Nunez something like, 'Can't you hear the path?' Like, when you walk, can't you hear the path?"

"Oh, right. Right."

"Yeah. Then he says, 'Do I have to lead you like a child?' Then...then Nunez laughs at him. He says, 'No, no. I don't have to hear the path. I can see it!' And then—here's the good part—the blind guy says, 'See! There's no such word as *see!*' Isn't that great? And I love it—I love it—when the blind guy says to Nunez, 'Okay, cut this silly shit out and follow me. You know, follow the sound of my footsteps."

"Yeah. I remember," Phil said.

"Okay. So here's what made me think. It's the Country of the Blind, right?"

"Right."

"What I mean—just...just for what I was thinking—countries have their own language. And sometimes some words from one language can't be translated into—I mean, there might be a word in one language and there's not a corresponding word in a different language. Like, the word *see* isn't in the language in the Country of the Blind."

"That's true."

Jenny became quiet. Suddenly, she jerked her eyes back to Phil. "And here's the thing!" Her hands were moving once again. "There's something about me being blind that's really different from sight. This never occurred to me before, so I'm not even sure what I'm talking about, but I think—I think, well...it's not just, like, it's not just that you can see and I can't. I've never seen. So I don't know what that's like."

Jenny paused. Her hands grew still. She grew pensive. Phil could see that she was deep in thought. "And even," she began speaking once again, "there's all this; it's funny. I mean, I'm still chasing sight. That's what it seems like. Chasing sight."

"What?" Phil said. "What do you mean?"

"I mean, since I was a kid, people have been telling me to *act sighted*. I actually practice acting sighted."

"Really?"

"Yeah! I'm constantly reminding myself that people can *see*, whatever the hell that is. So I say to myself, 'Smile. Make eye contact. Don't do anything rude, like touching the wrong thing.' And it goes on and on. So I'm wondering, am I like that woman, that blind woman? Remember? Nunez was pulling her out of the Country of the Blind when the mountains came crashing down. I know there was that mountain slide, or landslide, or whatever you call it. But still, Nunez, the sighted guy, was *pulling* her, pulling Medina-saroté out of the Country of the Blind and into where...? The Country of the Sighted?"

"Which way you going?" Jenny said as she stood.

"Oh. I'm walking up to Spadina."

"Oh. I'm going to Huron. Just the next block. But I can walk with you."

"Yeah, that's great."

Phil stood and joined her. He touched her lightly on her right arm with his left. She moved her hand down his arm and curled her fingers into his.

An Easy Walk

Brian couldn't remember a day, at least for the past couple of months, that he didn't feel a little anxious. And, as the days and weeks went on, he was feeling his anxiety more acutely. He was feeling anxious about this too, and this was making matters even worse.

Feeling anxious and then feeling anxious about being anxious—sometimes Brian just had to laugh. *What's wrong with me?* he often asked himself. He told himself to chill and settle down. *This is not such a big deal. Don't blow it out of proportion.* He gave himself this kind of criticism more and more as his days filled with anxiety went on.

Of course, Brian knew that his anxiety wasn't the kind that people talked about on television nowadays. He wasn't suffering from depression. He wasn't suffering from an anxiety disorder. *I am anxious, but not like that*, he thought. And yet the anxiety persisted—day after day, week after week.

The more he thought about it, the more he thought he had no reason to be anxious, and the more he thought about this, the more anxious he became. Brian was becoming thoroughly confused.

The only thing he could think of was that his eyesight, or, more precisely, what was happening to it, was making him anxious. His eyesight was getting worse and worse. It wasn't all that great to begin with. He had been legally blind for at least the past twenty years. *Legally blind.* This expression made him laugh. *As if you can be "illegally blind,"* he often mused. But in the last while, his eyesight, legally blind as it was, was getting worse—much worse.

Things seemed to be disappearing. Brian knew that they had been there. He just couldn't see them anymore. And the things he could see seemed smaller—not farther away, but smaller.

Shrinking. Things were shrinking. The world seemed to be shrinking, right in front of his eyes. The world was closing in on him. His eyesight was getting worse, and his world was getting smaller. Even though this made him anxious, Brian took some consolation in the fact that *the* world wasn't shrinking. It was only *his* that was. At least he wasn't confused about this. But recently, even *this* was getting more and more difficult for him to hang onto.

Brian thought of these things as he sat on the patio of a café on Harbord Street, waiting for Cora. He liked this café. It was one of those nice artsy cafés in Toronto's Annex neighborhood. It was also only a couple of blocks away from his apartment on Spadina Avenue. Getting to the café was, in his view, an easy walk. Out the front door of his apartment, turn right, right once more at the end of the block, and, a block and a half later, there it was—an easy walk.

As was his procedure, Brian arrived at that café at least thirty minutes before he had arranged to meet anyone. Whomever he was meeting wouldn't be there early. This was definitely not the artsy Annex way—to be fashionably late was. Brian could rely on this. This suited his legal blindness quite nicely. Whomever he was meeting would have to find him on the busy patio and not the other way around.

"Brian! Sorry I'm late!"

"Whoa! You scared me, Cora!"

"Sorry. Sorry. How're you doing?"

"I'm good."

Cora sat next to Brian even though it was a table for four. She always did this. Brian had told her he liked it. It was because he could hear her better. Cora organized her ever-present big bag of stuff under the table in front of her.

"There," she said. "So how are you?" She touched Brian's arm. "Sorry. Really. Sorry I'm late."

"You're always late. Don't worry about it."

"Okay. Okay. Can I bum a smoke?"

"Yeah, sure. I'm gonna put them right here between us, okay, Cora?"

"Cool. Honest, Brian, I'm gonna buy you a pack one day."

"Don't worry about it. Don't go buying cigarettes; otherwise you'll start smoking as much as I do. Just smoke mine."

"Okay. But I'm gonna buy you a beer."

"Deal. Hey, Cora...?"

"Yeah?"

"You gotta get your own ashtray."

"Oh, yeah. Forgot. Be right back."

She's quick, Brian thought as Cora grew smaller. He took a couple of deep breaths. He felt his heart speeding up and thought that breathing slowly might help. Cora just shrank out of view. Brian continued to breathe slowly.

"Got it. Oh! Did I scare you again? Sorry."

Cora eased into her chair and slowly pulled up to the table. She carefully placed the ashtray down on the table in front of her.

"There," she said. "Now you don't have to worry about getting burned."

"Actually, Cora, it's you I'm worried about; I don't wanna burn *you*."

"Well, it's all good. You don't have to worry about that."

"Good."

"You seem a little jumpy today. Just grabbin' a smoke. You okay?"

"Yeah—no. I'm good," Brian said.

"Good? We've been friends for, what, five years now?"

"About that."

"Five years. That's what I mean. I know when

you're good, Brian. You just seem a little jumpy, that's all."

"What can I get you?"

Brian flinched at the sound of the server's voice. She seemed to appear out of nowhere.

"Oh, right," Cora said. "I guess I should order something. You want that beer now, Brian?"

"No. Later. I'll have another coffee for now."

"That was a regular coffee, right?" the server said.

"Yeah. Oh, and a couple more sugars."

"You got it. And for you?"

"I think," Cora said, "cappuccino. Yeah, I'll have a cappuccino. Oh, with cinnamon. Oh, and sugar, too."

"Okay. Cappuccino with cinnamon and a regular coffee. I'll bring sugar and cream too."

Why he'd tried to hide things from Cora, Brian wasn't sure. He didn't know why he'd told her he was "good" when he wasn't. Especially since Cora knew he wasn't. She knew he was jumpy. And, what's more, she had known this for the past couple of months.

Brian had talked to Cora about how his legal blindness was turning into...into what? Into some realm beyond legality? He'd told her about how anxious this move, whatever it was, made him. Cora had responded in the way Brian thought she would.

"Oh, Brian," she'd said, "I know it's a drag. It's just that your sight seems to be changing. You're losing more of it. But, you know, it's no big deal.

You've done so well for so long with hardly any sight, so you'll be okay. And, you know...I'm right here with you. It's not the same, but I'm gonna go through it with you."

Cora had a way of bringing things down to earth. Brian liked that about her. After all, he felt the same way. *Yeah, it is a drag that I'm losing more of my sight*, he thought. *But no big deal. I can handle it. That's not what's making me anxious. I mean, I don't like it, but it's not making me anxious. I don't know what is. Something though....*

"You having another bad eye day? Is that why you're jumpy?" Cora said, interrupting his thoughts.

"Probably. Hey, Cora, where's my lighter?"

"Oh, shit! Sorry. Here. Back on your cigarettes."

"Thanks."

"I'm always forgetting. Sorry."

"It's okay. It's only been five years," Brian said, laughing.

Cora laughed too. "I know," she said. "It's like I'm never gonna learn."

Brian lit a cigarette and breathed deeply. He leaned back into his chair. "You're probably right, Cora. Just having a bad eye day."

"Well, guess you're gonna have a few of those. Mmm! This cappuccino is good."

"Guess so," Brian said.

"Yeah. Hey, Brian...?"

"Yeah?"

"Is there, uhhh, I mean, is there something else? I mean, lately...lately it seems like you've been a little down," Cora said. "I don't mean you shouldn't be," she quickly added. "You know, losing more sight. It's gotta be messing with your head a little bit."

"Yeah. I suppose," Brian said. "I can get around easily. Find, you know, places I wanna go, shit like that. That hasn't changed much. It's just that, uhhh...."

"It's just what?"

"I don't know, Cora. All right. Okay. It's like this.... I can still find my classes, teach them, go to faculty meetings, stuff like that. Right?"

"Okay."

"You know, still mark papers with my TA. So not much has changed."

"So..." Cora said slowly, "so it's just not...it's just not that you're having another bad eye day. Is it?"

"Not really...."

The café's patio was bustling. Voices—so many, so many different kinds of voices. Voices mingling with one another, intertwining, making a melodic yet unintelligible cacophony of sound. Chairs scraping on the concrete floor of the patio and the clinking sounds of cutlery and glasses joined the melody of voices in a contrapuntal harmony. The patio was bustling. And yet, somehow, Brian felt isolated from it. It was as though he wasn't a part of it, as though he wasn't contributing to it. He felt an eerie sense of separation.

"Okay," Cora said, waving her cigarette in the air as though punctuating a proclamation. "It's not a bad eye day."

"Put the lighter back, Cora."

"Jeez! I forgot again. There. So," she continued, "if not a bad eye day, what then? What's making you jumpy?"

"I dunno, Cora. It's sort of like—it's like things are far away, you know? No. Not far away. It's more like.... Okay. This is weird. It's like the world is getting smaller or something. Things seem more private. See, told you it was weird."

"Are you kidding?" Cora said. "Weird? I don't think so."

"I figured you'd say something like that," Brian said.

"Like what? I didn't say anything."

"Yet."

"Yet?" Cora said. "Yet? What did you think I was going to say?"

"Oh, I don't know. Write a novel about it."

Cora laughed. "Oh. She's on her way. Want another coffee or something?"

"I'll have that beer you owe me."

"So, you thought I was going to tell you to write a novel?" Cora said after the waitress deposited Brian's beer and the white wine she had ordered for herself.

"Yeah," Brian said. "Something like that."

"Why would you think that?" Cora said. "Actually, it's not a bad idea. But why do you think that?"

"See? You're always saying stuff like that."

"Like what?"

"Like, if something's bugging you, or even if something's wonderful or intriguing, you say, 'Write about it. Write fiction. Write creative nonfiction.' You're always saying that."

"Well, it's true," Cora said.

"See?"

"I know. But it's *true*, Brian. I mean, you know it is. Come on, you've been teaching Canadian lit for years?"

"Yeah. "

"So you know how beautiful novels are. Even short stories. You can say things in a story that you just can't say in those academic books you write."

"True," Brian said. "But you fiction writers still need critics."

"I know. This isn't a *competition*, Brian." Cora laughed. "I mean, this privacy thing you're feeling, or whatever it is—imagine creating characters, or even one character, who really *lives* this privacy. You could actually bring this privacy to life!"

"You can. I can't."

"You've been around good literature for a long time now. Of course you can."

"Right. That's what all great writers say. 'You

can write too.' That's what all you guys say."

"What? 'All you guys'?"

"I mean, guys like *you*, Cora."

"Like me? What are you talking about?"

"Come on, Cora. Get serious. You write novels. You're a Giller Prize winner, for Christ's sake!"

"So what? You're an English professor."

"Not the same thing."

"You know what I mean. You know as well as I do that literature engages with this kind of life stuff. It reveals it. It makes something of it. Remember, English prof? *Poiesis?* Writing isn't therapy, even though sometimes it can be therapeutic. It's *making stuff*! Bringing stuff alive! Fiction can take you places where life sometimes just can't!"

"How you guys doing? Another round?"

Brian flinched.

Cora said, "Sure. Another round."

There she goes again, Brian thought. Cora always did this. Literature is revealing. It's a making. *Poiesis.* She certainly could be pedantic at times. *But what do you expect from writers?* he thought. He just analyzed novels. He didn't write them. He's a critic, a theorist. *Where would novelists be without guys like him?* he wondered. Brian sensed something different today, though. Sitting on the patio with Cora, having a couple of drinks—she didn't seem quite as pedantic. Of course, it may have been him. Maybe he was listening a little differently today. Cora was right, he knew. He had to figure out this feeling of anxiety. Writing was as good a way as any, and that would certainly put the brakes on trying to analyze everything. *Now who's pedantic?* Brian thought.

People were just popping in and out of Brian's space, or so it seemed to him, but not in the way they ordinarily did. They were just there. Suddenly just there. It seemed to him that they just came out of—out of nowhere! The server was just there. She came out of nowhere. Cora, too, came out of nowhere. She was gone, and then she was there, with an ashtray! Brian knew that this was nonsense. The server didn't come out of "nowhere." She was always there, on the patio. Cora didn't come out of nowhere either. She went to get an ashtray and came back.

And yet....

Not into my life, Brian thought. *People weren't coming into my life. They were coming into...my world! Right! That's different!*

"...my mind. I don't think writing—no. Not writing."

"What? Sorry. What?" Cora's voice cut through the cacophony of patio sounds. Her words pierced his thoughts. It was as though they jerked him out of his thoughts or, perhaps, into them.

"Where were you?" Cora said.

"Oh! Sorry. Really. Sorry, Cora."

"Man, it was like you were far, far away—in some land where no Brian had gone before."

"I'm sorry, Cora. Really. I am. What were you saying?"

"Oh, nothing really that important. Actually, I was just saying—uh, it's just, I mean. I was just saying. Well, I think I changed my mind about you writing about this stuff."

"What stuff?" Brian said.

"Wow! You really *were* far, far away. The stuff we were talking about, Brian. You know, about your world—your world shrinking, getting smaller."

"Oh, right," Brian said. "But I thought you were all into...into me writing about it. I thought you were into me going places, like writing. Going places with writing—you know, places where life can't take you."

"Yeah. I know," Cora said. "But I was thinking about it. You know, when you were far, far away. I was thinking about it. I think I changed my mind, Brian."

"Changed your mind?"

"Yeah. You're right. I'm always saying, 'Write about this. Write about that.' But the more I think about it, the more I think...I think I'm changing my mind."

"Thank God."

"Don't be like that," Cora said. "It's just that—okay, listen."

"Okay, sorry. I'm listening."

"Again? Another round?"

Brian flinched again.

"Yeah. What do you think, Brian?"

"Yeah. Sure."

"Okay, be right back."

"Oh," Cora said. "This time I'll have a spritzer."

"Okay. And you? Another beer?"

"Yeah."

"Perfect," the server said. "Be right back." And she popped out of Brian's world as quickly as she had popped into it.

Write. Don't write, Brian thought. *First, she wants me to write about this stuff, and then she doesn't. My life. My world. Write. Don't write.* He felt as though his thoughts were coming undone, as though they were being split in two.

This was making him anxious.

"White wine spritzer," Brian said after the server had delivered their drinks. "*Ooooooh.*" He was trying to get his thoughts together, teasing Cora about her drink, buying some time. He could deal with this anxiety. *Lighten up,* he told himself. *Deal with it. It's no biggie.* And yet...this, too, was making him anxious.

"So, what were you saying about changing your mind?"

"Oh, right," Cora said. "Let me get a smoke first. Okay?"

"Yeah. Sure. Go ahead, Cora."

"All right," Cora said, waving her lighted cigarette in front of her as if urging her voice to speak. "This is what I was thinking."

"Cora. My *lighter.*"

"Damn! There. It's back."

"Thanks."

"Oh, don't mention it," Cora said. "Here's what I was thinking. I think you're right. Basically, you're not a writer. You're a...a...what did you say you were, Brian?"

"A critic."

"Right. A critic. I think you're right. I sometimes think that everyone can write...."

"Sometimes?"

"I know. I know. But now that I think more about it...maybe you shouldn't write about this stuff. Maybe *I* should."

"You! You should? *You* should write about *my* stuff?"

"Yeah," Cora said, punctuating her response with a curt wave of her cigarette. "Me."

"Yeah. So what happened with me writing fiction and going places far, far away where no life has gone before?"

"I thought you liked the idea about me changing my mind."

"I do. But I didn't think you were going to change it from *me* writing to *you* writing."

"Oh, don't be so melodramatic, *critic*. Don't be such a baby."

Brian laughed. He stubbed his cigarette out, picked up his pint of beer, and leaned back in his chair. "So, what did you have in mind, Cora?"

"Here's what I was thinking. You know, how I was saying before—you can handle it. You can handle losing more sight, Brian."

"Right."

"That's, like, adjusting," Cora said. "We all do that for one reason or another. I'm not saying it's easy to adjust. What I'm thinking is that adjustment...it's, uh, the *goal* of adjusting."

"Go figure," Brian said.

"No, no. Wait. Just hear me out."

"Okay."

"So you adjust. It might take a short time, a long time, but you adjust. It's not easy, but you do it. Then what? What do you have? You've got a well-adjusted life. Okay. But is that it? What happens to all that wonderful stuff, that stuff about your world shrinking? It's gone!"

"But that's a good thing," Brian said.

"I guess so," Cora said. "But where? Where did it go? It didn't just disappear like people in your world do, like you were saying they do. It's *somewhere*. I figure it gets buried under all that adjustment. I don't mean something psychoanalytic here, Brian, so...."

"Sounds like it," Brian said.

"Well, it might. But I don't mean it that way. What I mean is that you've got a whole world—a whole shrinking world—that's *buried*. I mean, that adjustment is keeping it from you. Actually, it's keeping it from all of us."

"All of us? Who's 'us'?"

"I dunno. I mean, all of us. All of us adjust stuff. All of us bury all kinds of worlds under adjustment. Then we get banal."

"Banal?"

"Yeah. It's, like, the big deal nowadays. *Get adjusted.* Actually, it's, like, *get normal.* You know that Tylenol ad? *'Get back to normal...whatever your normal is.'* It's like normal is the biggest deal in the world. Okay. I'm not saying we shouldn't be normal, or something like that. I'm saying that if that's all we are, it's kind of banal. Oh! Here's what it is! The *banality of normality!*"

Brian laughed once more. "I don't know what I'm laughing at, Cora. What you're saying isn't that funny. Actually, it's great. But it's still making me laugh."

"I know what you mean," Cora said, joining Brian in his laughter.

"It's almost as if you're saying that when we adjust to something, we try not to give it another thought," Brian ventured.

"Yeah."

"Like this world of mine—this shrinking world. If I adjust to it, I won't have to imagine it anymore."

"Exactly!" Cora said, lighting yet another one of Brian's cigarettes. "I put your lighter back, Brian."

Brian's laugh became almost hysterical.

"Okay. Listen," Cora said. "That's exactly what I mean. *Imagination!* We're not encouraged to *have* an imagination! We're supposed to get normal, get a job, yadda, yadda, yadda. Don't get me wrong. We need that stuff, but when we get it, imagination gets buried. See, Brian, that's why you critics need us. You need us fiction writers. We all do. Someone has to dig us out of that big mound of adjustment."

"Out of the banality of normality, right, Cora?"

"Yeah," she said, leaning back in her chair.

"How're we doing?"

Brian flinched.

"It's five-thirty already!" Cora said. "Man, I gotta go. You good, Brian?"

"Yeah. We'll take the bill."

"That was cheap," Cora said after she had paid for their drinks.

"Thanks. I'll get you next time, Cora."

"Don't worry about it. I'm headed to Bathurst Street. You okay?"

"Yeah. I'm fine. I'm just gonna go to the bathroom and head home."

They stood, hugged, and said goodbye.

"You okay to the bathroom?"

"Yeah. Yeah. I've been there a million times. I'm good."

"Okay. See you soon. Call me," Cora said as she popped out of Brian's world.

Brian turned to the table and leaned forward to retrieve his cigarettes and lighter. He noticed that he hadn't finished his beer. The bathroom could wait. He sat and lit a cigarette.

"Call me"—Brian knew Cora had spoken these words as she left the patio. And yet he was overcome with an eerie sensation. She was gone, literally gone, out of his world and still she spoke. They were her words and, somehow for Brian, they weren't. She was there, and yet not there. *Who else could have spoken these words?* he wondered. *No one. No one else. Cora spoke them.*

Her words came to Brian from a much farther distance than the width of the patio. *Perhaps*, he thought, *she spoke them to someone else.* Or perhaps it was someone else who spoke these words. But it was Cora who spoke, Brian knew. What he didn't know was where these words came from. He felt his spine tingle as he smoked his cigarette and sipped his beer. He shook his head quickly from side to side as though to drive these thoughts out.

So now she wants to write about my stuff. Brian figured that thinking about something else would make the eerie sensation he was feeling subside. And so while he finished his beer, he thought about Cora taking his stuff into the faraway land of fiction.

They seemed to be popping out at will and from everywhere. It seemed to Brian that as soon as he maneuvered around one table, another took its place. First one and then another. He didn't even see it coming! He had enough sight to see the tables as he approached them, but this time on the way to the bathroom, the patio tables seemed to be coming out of nowhere. He managed to avoid the tables and not to run into them. No one sat at the tables. No people! Just tables! One after another popping in front of him.

I don't remember this many tables! How many are there? They don't even look like tables. They have to be tables. What else could they be? Tables or not, things were popping into Brian's world. He couldn't seem to get off the patio and into the bar to the bathroom. He was shuffling more than walking. He made very little progress. It seemed to him as though tables were appearing and disappearing in front of him. They were popping in and out of his world. He was barely moving now.

The walk home won't be an easy one, he thought.

The Darkness

He was awake. Eli knew this though he was enveloped in a darkness that he didn't know. He tried to remember the darkness, its source.

The darkness waltzed through Eli, and he made a vague attempt to cobble together a memory from the bits and pieces of unsteady thought. It wasn't the darkness of night where light still lingered in ever-adapting eyes. It was the complete darkness of...of what? He couldn't remember.

Eli lay awake. Somewhere. In darkness.

And then it came to him. Suddenly. A bit of unsteady thought held fast by memory came to him.

Lights! Lights! Eli didn't see the lights. He was still completely surrounded by darkness. The lights were there, though—enveloped in the darkness—but they were there. He remembered. Eli remembered seeing these lights. Where? He wasn't seeing them now. He was still in the complete darkness of...? He still couldn't remember. He remembered the lights, though. He saw them somewhere before. Where and when?

The darkness didn't conjure up any memory of the kind of darkness it was. It gave Eli only lights—lights floating in the darkness that he couldn't remember.

Refocus, Eli thought. Focusing on the darkness instead of lights might dredge up a memory. He couldn't remember a darkness this complete. It wasn't the darkness of closed eyes, of night, of anything. It was *darkness* darkness. Just darkness.

Eli began to feel the darkness more and more. It surrounded him. Enveloped him. Held him. This darkness was not a memory. It wasn't obscuring anything. It was there. Real. Touching him. Not the darkness of a darkened room or of night or of anything he could remember. It was...darkness. It crept around him. It pressed against him, tightly, as though it wanted to get inside of him.

Eli rubbed his eyes. This brought back the lights. Was he remembering them? Was he seeing them this time? He didn't know. He decided to be still and start again.

All right, Eli thought. *Just be calm.* This darkness was like no other he had ever known. It was there and, somehow, it eluded his experience. He couldn't get it. He wasn't seeing it. He couldn't watch it. It wasn't as though he was seeing "in the dark." He wasn't even sure if it was darkness. It was definitely not like any darkness he had known, but it was there. Actually, it was everywhere. This, Eli knew.

Be still, Eli reminded himself. *Be still.*

I can't see because it's all dark. Eli tried to

apply this explanation to the situation. *Makes sense*, he thought. *If it wasn't dark, I would be able to see. No one can see in the dark. So far, so good.* The darkness was preventing him from seeing. He would be able to see if it wasn't so dark.

Darkness. Darkness. Man, that's all I can see. Nothing but darkness. But that's all there is to see.

Shit, Eli thought. *There goes that explanation. I can't see this darkness. This shit isn't like darkness. This darkness is not darkness. It's not all black. It's not pitch black. That, I could see. Pitch dark. Pitch black. That stuff, I can see. This dark...I can't see it. It's dark. It's not pitch anything; it's just dark!*

Eli was angry now—not heeding his own admonition to be still. Nothing made sense to him. It was dark, yet not. He could see it, yet couldn't. He knew it was dark, yet didn't. It just didn't make sense. *I'm losing my mind*, Eli thought. *There's nothing! Nothing! Nothing! But, shit, there's something! I can feel it!*

...And he could.

Eli felt the darkness as it pressed in on him. He thought it was trying to penetrate—no...not penetrate. The darkness was trying to seep into him, and not just in one place, not just into his chest, his abdomen, not even into his head, or his brain. It was seeping in everywhere. Head-to-toe darkness. It was seeping, very slowly, into all of him.

Eli squirmed and turned in his bed the best he could, trying to escape the seeping darkness. And yet it kept seeping into him. Seeping. Seeping. Very slowly, seeping. He twisted and turned. "*No!*" Eli screamed. "*No!*" But the darkness kept coming in.

Eli needed to get out of bed, get out of here and run. He tried to sit up, but he fell back on the pillow. His left arm felt funny. He tried to prop himself up on his right elbow. Again, he fell back onto the pillow.

Eli screamed and threw his right arm violently to the side. It hit something, something like a table. It moved. Things crashed to the floor, hard things that bounced, and he heard the sound of breaking glass. He screamed again.

Eli turned wildly to his left. Something was stuck into the back of his left hand. He couldn't believe it. "*What the fuck!*" he screamed. He grabbed the thing and yanked. He threw it violently, and something rolled, crashing into something else. Eli screamed again.

A door was flung open. "*Eli. Eli.*" A voice, a woman's voice. It sounded to Eli as if she were shouting, and yet her shouting was gentle. "*Eli,*" she gently shouted. "It's okay. It's okay. I think you had that dream again. Just lie back. There you go."

"It was no dream this time," Eli shouted. "This time, honest, this time it was real. The darkness just comin' in me. It's *still* comin' in me."

"You're okay," the woman said. "Everything's okay."

"Oh, man." Eli was sobbing now.

"It's okay, hun. You ripped your IV out. I'll call for a new one, and we'll hook it up again. We'll get some more of that sedative you like so much."

"No, no. I don't want that shit no more. It wasn't a dream this time. It was real. Real. The darkness is gettin' into me."

The woman spoke quietly into a device that resembled a small cellphone.

"Man, Tony. Fuckin' great to be back here again."

"No shit, Eli."

"Hey, man, where, uh, where Sally? Where Justin? They don't work here no more?"

"No, no. They're still here. They start at seven. You know, they're on that seven to close shift."

"Cool. Dey gonna be surprised to see me."

"Yeah. They sure will."

"Seven? You say they comin' at seven?"

"Yeah."

"What the time now, man?"

"Uh," Tony said, looking at his watch, "it's about twenty to. Hey, Eli, what happened to that fancy talking watch of yours?"

"Man, you know what happened to that watch, Tony?"

"What?"

"That day. That day. That watch. It got all

smashed up that day."

"God. You know, Eli, I thought you were dead. I thought you got killed. I really did."

"Nah. Nah. Ain't no little car accident gonna kill this negro."

"I know. But *jeezus*, Eli. You were just lying there—lying there in the street. Your head was all bleeding. You weren't moving. Shit, you were unconscious. I thought you were *dead*."

"Ain't you never heard of these cats—you know, these cats—the ones they got *nine* lives. Ain't you never heard that?"

"Right. I suppose you're one of those cats. Right?"

"Sure is, man. Sure is."

"Yeah. You're macho, all right. You're macho."

"Yeah. Yeah, I'm macho, all right," Eli said, quietly. "Come on, Tony. Cheers, man," he said, recapturing some of his exuberance.

Eli picked up his pint of beer and held it to Tony, and listening to their clink, he said, "Cheers, man."

"Cheers, Eli."

They both chuckled, but a sound that was more an extended and knowing sigh came from their lips. Then...they sank back into their own thoughts.

Eli walked positioned on Tony's right, his left hand resting on the back of Tony's wheelchair. His right hand swept the sidewalk in front of him. Left to right, right to left, back and forth—sweeping in front of him, his white stick in hand, he moved in a rhythm that had become so automatic to him.

They were walking down South Wabash Street in Chicago, the Windy City, the town in which they both lived. Why they were doing so was unclear to Tony. It was Eli's decision—and an impetuous one—to leave the bar before Justin and Sally arrived to begin their shift.

"Let's go, Tony," Eli had said suddenly.

"What? Where?" Tony had replied, just as suddenly.

"Come on, man. Let's go. Let's get out of here."

"I don't get—"

"Let's just go," Eli said brusquely. "I'm dropping a twenty on the table." He was standing now. "That'll cover it."

"All right, all right," Tony replied, slightly irritated.

And now they were walking down South Wabash.

"What the fuck was the rush, man?" Tony asked.

"Tell ya in a minute. Keep your shirt on, okay?"

"Okay!" Tony remained irritated. "Where the hell we goin'?"

"Just up the street. We goin' to Legends. Just two blocks up."

"Great. Any particular reason for going there?" Tony said sarcastically.

"We just goin'. Tell ya when we get there. Just keep rollin'."

"Fine."

"See," Eli said. "Ain't this nice? Got a little blues playing in the back. Live stuff don't start 'til ten. We be gone by then. No cover. Ain't it nice?"

"Yeah, it's nice. But why the fuck you wanted to get out of that bar so fast? It's like someone lit a fire under your ass."

"Hey, just chill, Tony. I just gots ta get outta there, that's all. Come on, man. Chill. Cheers, Tony."

They clinked their glasses.

Tony decided to remain quiet and not say anything. *Fuck him*, he thought. *I'm not gonna say a word. Chill? Yeah, fuck.*

"I just looove Buddy Guy's Legends Blues Club. You?" Eli's words flowed into Tony's silence that was boiling.

"Yeah, I like it," Tony said. "Don't know what the fuck we're doing here. But I like it."

"I just need to chill, man. Dunno. Wanted nobody hearin' what I'm sayin'. Just chill. Relax. Den I need t'talk some shit out witchya. Meantime...meantime, we let these blues just waaash over us. Okay, man?"

"Yeah. Okay," Tony said.

Despite his frustration, Tony really liked this blues club. He liked it from the moment he rolled in,

Eli holding onto the back of his titanium wheelchair. He noticed all the blues memorabilia, guitars mostly, as he and Eli moved through the club. They rolled by a glass case displaying a jean jacket that was ripped in several places. *Bob Dylan's jacket*, Tony read on the plaque as they rolled by. He was very impressed. *Gotta roll around later, look at these guitars and see who they belonged to*, he thought.

"Find a table where no one's sittin' close," Eli told him, and so he did.

Tony sat in his chair across from Eli, sipping a beer and looking at him. Still, even after fifteen minutes or so, not a word passed Eli's lips. *Chilling*, Tony thought. *Fuck.*

Impatience now joined Tony's frustration. It wasn't that he didn't understand. He did. Being hit by a car, knocked out, and taken to a hospital by an ambulance—that was serious shit. Tony knew this, and he understood that it would rattle anyone. Shit. He was there. He saw the accident happen. And it rattled the shit out of *him*. It would rattle the shit out of anyone, *especially a blind guy*. Tony had seen Eli standing at the curb, his white stick moving slightly from the curb to the street, and then, suddenly, Eli stepped off the curb. Tony shuddered at the memory.

And yet Tony's impatience and frustration were now all mixed together, all stirred up, and this mixing and stirring yielded: *pissed off!* He was pissed off. His being "pissed off" and his "understanding" were now beginning to engage in a battle inside of him. He felt it in his gut. *Can't hold out much longer*, he thought.

"Eli."

"What?"

"You been sitting there for hours, quiet as a mouse, not saying a word."

"Shit. Hours? Not hours. Only minutes."

"Whatever," Tony said. "You're so quiet it's getting a little eerie in here. What the fuck is going on? What's up?"

"Oh, man—chill. Ain't nuttin'."

"Nothing!" Tony's voice was now several decibels higher than it had been just moments ago.

"Shhh!" Eli said, leaning forward in his chair. "Come on, man. Easy. Don't be yellin' so the world can hear. A'right?"

"All right, all right. But, Eli! What's going on? You're sitting there all quiet, sombre, like you're way off in the distance, thinking about something. I know you are. What's that shit you wanted to talk about? Remember? You said you had some shit to talk out."

Eli leaned back in his chair. He tapped his fingers on the side of his pint of beer, drumming to the beat of the blues song playing in the background. The truth was that he was thinking about those dreams he was having, if they were dreams. He was thinking about the darkness, if it was darkness. The trouble was that he didn't know what to think, or even how to think about it. It *was* darkness. But it wasn't any kind of darkness that he knew.

"Okay. Listen, Tony." Eli leaned forward once again, and this time so did Tony. "Listen. See, it's that accident." He cleared his throat. "See, after the accident...."

"Yeah?"

"I was in the hospital for, like, a week."

"I know. I came to see you a couple of times, remember?"

"Yeah. Yeah, I know. I know. All right, here's the thing. 'Member one time when you were visiting me and I told you about that dream I was havin' about darkness?"

"I do. I remember. You were telling me about nightmares, about the nightmares you were having. Right?"

"Yeah. Well, not ezacly."

"What do you mean 'not exactly'?"

"Like this. It's like this. See, I don't think—I mean, I don't think it was nightmares."

Eli looked down at the pint of beer that he was now clutching in both hands, saying nothing. Tony did the same. Eli was trying to figure out how to continue. Thinking about his dream, if it was a dream, was very difficult. Talking about it bordered on the impossible.

Tony wasn't about to interrupt Eli's silence. He knew that Eli would speak soon. He knew, too, that this time he could be patient enough to wait for a few more minutes.

"Okay." Eli looked up and fixed his gaze on Tony. "Here's the thing. That dream, man. That dream, Tony. I don't think it's no dream."

"You mean that dream you told me about? That dream about darkness? That nightmare? You saying that wasn't a dream?"

"Yeah. I'm *sayin'*...I'm sayin' I don't think it's no dream. Honest, man. It's too real. I know...I know.... No need for you to say it. Some dreams, they seem real."

"Yeah," Tony said. "Some dreams are like that."

"I know. I had dreams like that before. But this one's *different*."

"What are you saying, Eli?"

"I'm *sayin'*...." Eli fell into silence once again, but this time for only a few moments. "I'm sayin'... I'm sayin' it ain't no dream. I *had* it, and I was *awake*!"

"*Really?*"

"Yeah. I mean it, man. I was wide awake. I know I was. And the dream, it came. But it— was—no—dream. Real, man—it was real."

"Fuck! Oh, man, Eli."

"It's crazy, man. I'm awake, wide awake. Last time—last time I'm sittin' on my couch, wide awake, and then it comes. The darkness comes. It comin' all in me! Comin' in everywhere!"

"Even in the hospital? Awake?"

"Yeah. Even in the hospital, couple times."

"Did you tell the doctors?"

"Doctors. What the fuck doctors know?"

"Eli. You gotta tell the doctors. What are you?

Some kind of big tough guy? 'How you doing?' the doctor asks you. 'Oh, cool, man,' you say. 'I'm cool. I'm Eli, big macho man. Ain't nuttin' wrong with me. Under control.' That's fucked up, Eli."

"Nah. Not a macho thing. I kinda told the doctors."

"Kinda? What's that supposed to mean?"

"Okay. Nurse. I kinda told the nurse."

"Kinda? What'd you say?"

"The dream—see, it happened once, right there in the hospital. But this time I was *awake*. Wide awake. Wasn't no dream. It was real. The darkness start...start comin' all in me. It fucked me up, man. Didn't know what was goin' on. Dreamin'. Not dreamin'. I guess I started yellin'. Knockin' shit around, too. Then the nurse come in. But I didn't know where I was. I be all fucked up. I just start yellin' and knockin' shit around. Then someone start holdin' my shoulders, sayin' shit."

"What kind of shit?"

"You know, like, 'take it easy,' 'chill,' shit like that. Then she start pushin' my shoulders—not hard, just a little bit. She tell me real easy like, you know, tell me to lie down, take it easy. Then she callin' someone, you know, on that little radio or whatever the fuck it is. She's sayin', 'Bring a sedative, bring an IV, room 506.' She talkin' like that."

It took him a little while, but Eli was able to locate the urinal. He hadn't been at Legends recently.

Three, four months ago, maybe, was the last time he was there. Still, after Tony gave him directions to the restroom, he remembered and he found the urinal.

Eli stood in front of the urinal, pissing and pissed off. He knew why he was pissing, but he wasn't sure why he was pissed off. He then made his way back from the restroom to the table without much difficulty. It seemed as though being pissed off returned to him a sense of confidence—a confidence he now embraced as one might an old friend from the past. Pissed off and confident—he felt both now, but he wasn't sure why he was pissed off.

"No problem finding everything in the can?"

"Smooth, baby. It goes smooth. I come here all the time before. Took me no time to get reeeee-familiarized."

"Cool."

"Hey, Tony, you pick a place to sit close to the john on purpose, right?"

"Yeah. You said pick a table, and so as I'm wheeling through, I see the can and then I see a table close by. I figure, hey, this is handy. I'm gonna grab it."

"You know—you know, the fuckin' thing is...I'm thinkin'...I'm thinkin' you might have some difficulty fittin' that titanium chair of yours into the, you know, into the stall."

"You think so?"

"I can't 'member now ezacly, but I'm thinkin',

uh, I'm thinkin' maybe, maybe not."

"We'll deal with that when the time comes," Tony said.

"All right, man. We handle it."

"Yeah. We got it," Tony said. "Hey, and Eli?"

"What?"

"You're looking lots better than before, you know, before in that other bar. Man, you fired outta there so fast, and I'm thinking...I'm thinking, *What the fuck?* You're looking more relaxed now. What happened in the other place, Eli? Like, we roll in here. We sit. Well, you sit. Then you go take a piss, get back, and you're all relaxed. Did you have to piss before? They got a pisser in the other bar, you know."

Eli and Tony laughed. Their laughter grew in intensity until it reached a crescendo. It then moved but in the opposite direction. They were now laughing sporadically, gasping.

"Before" was now coming back to them. They were now remembering, not speaking about, but remembering the old times, the good times, from before. Before, they laughed and laughed often. They laughed in the other bar and in other places too. They sat now, gasping, tears caressing their cheeks, and felt like they did—before.

"I thought you were pissed off," Tony said, still gasping.

"I *am* pissed off! I be pissed!" Eli said, gasping too.

"You sure sound it."

"*Phew!*" Eli said, removing his shades and rubbing tears from his eyes. "It's fuckin' hilarious!"

"What is?"

"I'm fuckin' pissed! Don't know why. I be fuckin' pissed and don't know what I be pissed at!"

"That's fuckin' hilarious!" Tony said.

And their laughter turned and began making the journey, once more, to its crescendo.

"All right," Eli said. "Prob'ly is a good thing you make us come back to this here bar, Tony."

"Well, yeah, you know—you know, you fired out of this bar before like your ass was on fire. I don't know what the hell's going on. We get to Legends. You go piss. You come back all pissed off, then...then we're laughing our heads off. So, I figure, we come back here. Besides, I gotta piss. So what the fuck. I figure, let's come back here so I can piss."

"Yeah, right. I *bet* you need to piss be the reason we back here."

"Whatever."

"Tony?"

"Yeah?"

"Glad we back here, man. Glad you make us come back."

"Wellllll look what the cat dragged in. I haven't seen you two guys for ages. Where ya been?"

"Sally! That be you?" Eli said.

"Who else?"

"Well, glad you still here."

"Yeah. Me too," Tony said.

"Let me grab you a couple...you still drinking the same thing? All right. I'll grab the beers. Be right back. Then you guys have to tell me where the hell you been."

"Jeez, it's good to see her," Eli said.

"Sure is," Tony said. "It's funny, Eli. We've been here, like, before—maybe three, four, maybe five times—and it seems like, you know, it seems like, I dunno, like we're kinda close to her or something."

"Yeah," Eli said. "Some folks, you know, some folks is just like that. Some folks is just friendly. I don't mean just, like, friendly, but *friendly*. Know what I'm sayin'?"

"True."

Sally returned with their beers. "There you go," she said. "Right in front of your right hand, my friend."

Eli lifted his pint of beer and nodded toward her. "Sally, my sister, cheers."

Sally gently put her hand on Eli's shoulder and said, "And cheers to you, my brother. Welcome back."

"Okay. I got a couple minutes here," Sally said as she approached their table. "So tell me. Where the hell you been, Eli?"

"Aw. Nuttin' much. Ain't much to it."

Tony's eyes met Sally's. She saw in his eyes

that Eli was downplaying and possibly even hiding something important.

"Two months back, two months...."

"Two!" Sally said. "More like three, Eli."

"All right. All right. *Three*," Eli mocked. "Three months ago, I had me a little *accident*."

"What happened? What kinda accident?"

"A little accident?" Tony interrupted. "Eli! You got hit by a fucking car!"

"You're shittin' me!" Sally said.

"All right. Okay. Don't freak. Got hit by a car. Took to a hospital. And now I'm good. End of story."

"End of story!" Sally said. "Three months! You were in the hospital three months?"

"No. I been there only a week. I...then I spend the rest of the time reeecuperatin'. Come on, Sally. Ain't I lookin' good? Not as good as you. That's for sure. But I back. I back allll together. Same old Eli."

"Thank God." Sally touched Eli on the shoulder once again. "Back in a few minutes. Oh, bring y'all a couple more?"

"Don't be lookin' at me all like dat, man."

"Looking like what?" Tony said. "You can't even see me."

"I can see you all right, lookin' at me all like dat."

"Like what?"

"Like you sayin', 'Hey, Eli, why you tell Sally?

Why you tell her?'" Eli was mocking Tony now. "'Uhhhh, ain't nuttin' to it, just had me a leetle car accident. In the hospital a week, recupe, and den...den, ah, be back. Same old Eli.' I hear you lookin' like dat, all sarcastic-like."

"Yeah, but, Eli...."

"What am I s'posed to say, man? 'Oh, *Sally*, I been in a *horrible* accident.' Am I s'posed to say that? I'm s'posed to say, 'Oh, Sally, d'darkness is all in me. I be different now. Not the same old Eli.' I'm s'posed to say that?"

"But...."

"Come on, man. Cheers, Tony."

They clinked their glasses.

They sat quietly. Their eyes met. They knew this. Both of them knew this. When Eli broke the silence, it was with a serene voice—serene words.

"Hey, Tony, you ever feel your chair? Like...like if it be...comin' all in you?"

The Bougie Girl

Muay Thai. Jesus Christ, Muay Thai.

She was recalling the time, three months or so ago, the time when Keira talked her into taking "Moy-Tie" lessons, or whatever the hell you called it. "Come on, Jenny," Keira had said to her. "It'll be good for you. It's great exercise. It's so fun. Pluuus, it's so good for movement and balance."

"Yeah, right. Good for you...balance...movement...sooo fun. Yeah, right. It's ridiculous. It's bullshit." Jenny always recalled that time in this way. It was not that Keira talked her into it; she *hassled* her, *nagged* her into it. "Okay. Okay." Jenny remembered how she finally gave into her. "Before you have a stroke or something."

Jenny also recalled how she had stormed out of the Muay Thai "centre," or whatever the hell you called it. Three months ago, disgruntled and humiliated, she was outta there—out the door and down the sidewalk, Keira on her heels.

"Jenny! Come on..." Keira had said back then. "This is only the second time," she reasoned. "Give it a chance," she said. "Come on. You're doing okay," she said. Jenny kept walking—walking as fast as her white cane would carry her.

"Jenny, *stop*! You're going to hit the sign!" Keira screamed these words at her. And Jenny did stop.

Then she and Keira stood there—stood there, toe to toe, shouting. Keira was shouting, trying to talk Jenny into going back to the gym, and Jenny was shouting, "Not in a million fucking years!" They were standing on the sidewalk in Toronto's busy Kensington Market. They were shouting at each other.

"Stop screaming at me!" Keira had said. "Everyone's gonna think I'm abusing a blind chick. Stop!"

"You are!" was Jenny's rejoinder. She spun on her heel and began walking, quickly.

Keira was only a few feet behind her, an exasperated look on her face, when Jenny suddenly stopped. She wondered why.

Jenny was disoriented. Her directions were all mixed up. And, what's more, it was Keira's fault. "You messed me up, got me all mixed up. Am I going the right way?" Jenny was still shouting.

Keira had told her that, in fact, she was not all messed up. "You're going in the right direction."

Jenny stood in the middle of the living room in her Huron Street apartment. She was going through some Muay Thai moves she had learned during those two lessons she had taken a few months ago. Punching the air, kicking it, she was trying to remember those moves. She didn't think that she remembered how to do them properly, but she continued to punch and kick the air. She was enjoying herself.

This is *good for my balance*, she thought as she punched and kicked. *Keira was right.* And, to Jenny's surprise, she was having fun.

"Swing, kick, and punch!" she shouted. She had spun and kicked the air. She began to lose her balance but quickly regained it and righted herself. *Man*, she thought, gasping a little, *that can't be the right way to do that.* She laughed and began to focus on regaining her sense of direction.

"No. The point is not that you were right," Jenny said.

"No?" Keira said.

"No!"

"Really? What then, Jenny? You just decided, allll by your little ol' self, that Muay Thai *is* good for you? Is that what happened? Hey? Huh?"

"Something like that," Jenny said.

"And don't think for one minute that I don't believe you!" Keira said.

"Hey, Keira, you want some more coffee? I'm gonna order."

Keira caught the server's eye.

Jenny and Keira didn't frequent this high-end café on Bloor Street West. It was across the street from the University of Toronto. They were both studying for their undergraduate degree in English. Undergraduate students didn't frequent this particular café. They knew that pretentious graduate students *did*. So, on those infrequent occasions, when they felt particularly "bougie," and felt the urge to mock pretentious graduate students, they would come to this café and order Americanos. Or cappuccinos. This is what pretentious graduate students, *the bougies*, did. Today, it was Americanos.

Jenny and Keira took pleasure in participating in the café's little bougie pretentiousness. They enjoyed spooning sugar into their Americanos. They used a fancy sugar container—fair trade, organic raw sugar, no less—with its own little sugar spoon. No little packets of white sugar for them. They made a show of pouring cream into their Americanos from an actual china jug. No plastic creamers for them. They then stirred their coffee with shiny spoons instead of brown plastic stir sticks.

Jenny and Keira would drink their Americanos and listen to these bougie graduate students speak. Or would drink cappuccinos. Sometimes they even drank lattes. They took pleasure in mimicking those students. They would throw words such as *deconstruction* and *post-structuralism* at each other, loud enough for these bougie graduate students to hear. They would also name-drop Derrida and Butler and others. They enjoyed this game to the hilt.

But, today, for some reason, it was different. Today it was Muay Thai only.

"See, Keira, you're good at Muay Thai. You're an expert. You go to Ohio—"

"Iowa."

"Whatever. You go there, and you win the belt!"

"I know, but—"

"So, Keira, me. So you're saying I should take Muay Thai and then I can become...*the Bliiiiind Womennnnn's Muay Thai Champion of the Worrrrrld!*"

Keira laughed. "That would be so cool," she said. "Can you imagine if there were such a thing? *Aaaand ladiiiiiess and gentlemennnn: the Bliiiiind Womennnnn's Muay Thai Champion of the Worrrrrld...! Jennyyyyy Daaaaawsonnnnn!*"

"Very funny!" Jenny said.

"Hey, Jenny! Check this out. *Ladiiiiiies and Gentlemennnnn: the Bliiiiind and Siiiiighted Muay Thai Tag-Team Champions of the Worrrrrld...! Jennyyyyy Dawsonnnnn and Keiraaaaa Heinnnnn!*

They were both laughing and enjoying the prospect of the two of them being Muay Thai champions.

"It's like this," Keira said. "Like this. Bend your knees a little. Okay, just rock gently up and down—and relax."

They were in Jenny's living room. Keira was

instructing her, demonstrating a basic Muay Thai stance.

"Like this?" Jenny said as she rocked gently on the balls of her feet, knees slightly bent.

"Yeah. Great. See, Jenny? Can you feel it? Can you feel how balanced you are right now?"

"Yeah."

"Okay. Now you're balanced. So now—now you can—you're ready to punch or kick, even a swing kick."

Keira then assumed the basic Muay Thai stance that she had just demonstrated to her. Jenny stood behind her just to her left side. Her right hand was on her shoulder and her left hand was on her knee, just as Keira had instructed her. In slow motion, Keira demonstrated the swing kick.

"Now you try it."

Jenny stood in front of her, gently rocking on the balls of her feet, perfectly balanced.

"Okay, Jenny. Nice...and slow."

In slow motion, Jenny performed a swing kick.

"Yeah! Perfect, Jenny! And, see, you're right back in position. Now another one, this time quicker.... Yeah! And, look, you're right back in position. Balanced."

"Oh, man! That feels *good*," Jenny said. "I'm balanced, Keira. I know exactly where I am!" She pointed. "Couch, right?"

"Exactly! Right on!"

"Two Americanos, please."

"No, wait. I'll have a latte."

"A *latte*. Ooooh, Jenny!"

They were back at the graduate student café. They were quiet, listening to the pretentious graduate students, waiting for their coffees to be brought to their table. There was some postmodern critique of...something or other.... Keira didn't catch the last words of what she overheard. She tapped Jenny's hand.

"I know," Jenny whispered. "I heard. Funny, eh?"

Their coffees arrived. They made their usual show of the fancy sugar bowl, the little china cream jug, and the shiny spoons.

"I really think what we need is a Derridean deconstruction analysis of art conceived as 'martial,'" Jenny said, mocking the bougie graduate students.

"I think that we need to explore—I mean, in a postmodern way—the *différance* that exists in the Third Space that exists between art and the martial."

"Uh-huh! *Différance* together with liminality would provide for the possibility of an intersectional, critical martial art."

"I think so, Jenny. It would also occasion the cultivation of a radical martial art."

Keira began laughing, and soon Jenny joined her.

They were enjoying their game of mocking

graduate students, but something hovered between them, unspoken. Their laughter subsided. And they sipped their coffees.

"Mmmm."

"You know what, Jen?"

"What?"

"Something's been bugging me."

"Bugging you? Like what?"

"Okay, Jenny. Like, okay—like, I don't wanna make a big federal case out of it...."

"Federal case out of what? Come on, Keira, spit it out."

"Okay. Here it is.... Remember, a few months ago, you went flying out of the Muay Thai gym that I took you to?"

"Yeah."

"Well, you were really pissed off...."

"But, Keira.... I know, but...."

"No, no. I know. Yeah, I understand why you were pissed off. I mean, you missed that punch completely. That would piss anyone off."

"I know."

"See, it's not that. I mean, I get pissed off every fucking day in the gym. You know, you miss a punch, you lose your balance, all that stuff. Yeah, I get it."

"Yeah. Man, I remember. I was *really* pissed off. Honest, Keira. The guy said—that coach, remember?—he says, 'I'm right in front of you, like two feet. Okay, Jenny,' he says, 'just jab. Left hand. Jab to my face.'"

"Yeah, I remember."

"And then...and then I started to move just a little to my left and forward, and just as I was moving my left hand to jab him—a little off balance...I just got a little off balance. I, like, fell! He had to *catch* me! I was so fucking pissed!"

"Yeah, I know. But, Jen, remember, you said...you also said that it was humiliating. You were humiliated."

"I remember that, Keira. It was, like, you know, so embarrassing. I was so embarrassed."

"Embarrassing to the point of *humiliation*? Right!"

"Right. I guess so. I mean...I don't mean, like, I humiliated myself. So I don't mean the guy, the coach—it's not exactly like he humiliated me. I humiliated myself."

"You mean by losing your balance?"

"Yeah. I lost my balance. I mean, come on. You have to be *balanced*."

"But, Jen, we all lose our balance. And if you're doing Muay Thai...."

"Yeah, see, like, '*We alllll lose our balance*,' like, '*We alllll.*' That's my point: 'We all'—blind or sighted—'we all lose our balance.'"

"Well, it's true."

"Maybe, Keira, but when you're blind and lose your balance, it's humiliating."

"That's bullshit!"

"No, really, Keira. When you're sighted and lose your balance, it's, like, well, we all do, especially if we're doing Muay Thai or not paying attention or something."

"What are you saying? When you're blind, it's different?"

"Okay. Okay. I know what you're saying. But when you lose your balance in Muay Thai, or whatever, it's just, like, well, 'Keira lost her balance. We all do.' Your coach starts giving you more instructions to show you how to keep your balance. Right?"

"Yeah, so?"

"Well, soooo...when you're blind, it's *your blindness*! That's what makes you lose your balance. What kind of instruction is the coach gonna give *me*? What's the coach gonna do, Keira? 'Oh, we'll cure your blindness, then you won't lose your balance.'"

"I get it. But there's something not right about what you're saying."

"That's probably true. But why the hell's a blind person doing Muay Thai anyway? Why put yourself in a position to be humiliated?"

Keira fell silent, and so did Jenny. They fingered their coffee cups and looked around at nothing. An ironic pall of embarrassment settled on their table.

"You know," Jenny said, breaking the silence, "it seems like I'm always putting myself in a spot to be humiliated. I mean, not even Muay Thai, but little things, like simple things."

"Like what?" Keira said.

"Little things. Okay, like, for example, I go into

Shoppers, you know, the drug store on Bloor and Walmer?"

"Yeah."

"The door there is pretty easy for me to find. There's sort of a big step there."

"Right. Oh, yeah."

"So then I go in the door—there's two doors there, but pretty easy to find both of them. Anyway, I go in the door, then someone says, 'Oh, can I help you?' 'Oh, no,' I say, 'I'm just gonna find the cashier and then I'm okay. It's fine,' I say. 'I can do it.' So I kinda have an idea—I mean, a pretty good one—where the cashier is. You and I were there before. Remember?"

"Yeah, we were."

"Okay, so I'm in the door. I take three...maybe four steps, and then there's that—I dunno what it is, a counter or something."

"Yeah."

"Then I make a couple right-hand turns, and there's the opening for the cashier's counter."

"Okay."

"Well, it's okay, *unless*...."

"Unless what?"

"Unless your shoulder hits a fucking—what's that thing called, with the, like, stuff on it?"

"A display?"

"Yeah. A display. You hit a display with your shoulder, and all the stuff falls on the floor. Big crash! Stuff everywhere! And guess what stuff fell?"

"What?"

"Batteries! Batteries. The fucking thing I was going there to buy—batteries! I was so humiliated!"

"Oh, so, Little Miss Independent, Little Miss I Can Do It Myself, knocks some shit over."

"Oh my God. Yeah. So embarrassing. So humiliating."

"But you didn't lose your balance, did you?" Keira said.

"Very funny," Jenny said.

"I'm not even gonna tell you that sighted people knock shit over too."

"Please."

"Okay. Okay. I'm just kidding. But don't you see the irony?"

"Irony? What irony?"

"You knocked over the very thing you went in there to buy."

"That's not irony. That's humiliation," Jenny said.

"Okay, listen. You went to Shoppers to buy batteries, right?"

"Yeah."

"So you needed batteries for one of those techie things you use for school or something. Right?"

"Yeah, for that little Dictaphone I like to make notes on."

"Right. So then you walk into Shoppers alllll independent-like, okay? And then Little Miss Independent smacks into something and knocks it over, and it's the very thing she want to buy."

"Very funny. And so what am I supposed to do? Laugh?"

"Exactly! So what happened? Did the cashier or someone come over and say something?"

"Yeah. She comes over. I think it was the cashier. Yeah, it was. She comes over, calls me 'dear.' Can you believe it? 'Dear.' Then she says, 'Everything is okay, dear. It's okay. It's just some batteries, that's all,' she says. 'No problem,' she says."

"And you're embarrassed, right?"

"Humiliated! Humiliated!"

"Okay. Okay. Humiliated. But don't you get it, Jenny? Irony! It's ironic! You went in for batteries, and you knocked the batteries over. So, fine, you're humiliated. But where's your balance?"

"Balance? What are you talking about?"

"You know what I'm talking about. You balance your embarrassment—"

"Humiliation."

"Humiliation. You balance your humiliation with irony. And then you have humour."

"Humour?"

"Yeah, humour. But you have to see how funny it is. And then you have to show the cashier how funny it is."

"You're kidding."

"No. You need balance. Okay, it's like this."

"Boy, I can hardly wait to hear this."

"Just listen then, Jenny. I'll come halfway.

— *153* —

Okay, sometimes I get it. Being blind is embarrassing—"

"Humiliating."

"Humiliating, then. But that's when you need balance. Like this. I knock batteries over at Shoppers. And, you know, it could be embarrassing, causing a scene and all that shit. Wait! Let me finish! But if it's *humiliating*, then you need to balance it with irony and then humour. See, 'cause I think—I think...I mean, I don't think you're embarrassed by your *blindness*, are you?"

"No. I'm not embarrassed. I'm not even humiliated. I only feel that way when I do something—you know, something stupid. And then I think, *Well, I wouldn't do that if I could see.*"

"But you might."

"Okay, I'll give you that. I might. But if I did that—you know, knocked the batteries over, if I could see—all they're gonna say is, 'Look at that clumsy chick.' They're not gonna feel sorry for me. They're not gonna say, 'Oh my God, that poor girl! She knocked the batteries over.'"

"Okay. But that's what I mean. If I knock something over, I think, *Shit, Keira, you're clumsy.* But here's the thing. If I'm alone and knock something over, no problem. If anyone else sees me, then it's a different story. Okay, I knock something over. Right?"

"Right."

"And I think, *Keira, you're fucking clumsy.* Then there's someone else there, and I think, *Oh my God, they think I'm clumsy too*, and that's when I get embarrassed."

"I know what you mean, Keira. I really do. But sometimes—sometimes it just feels like...like I have to be perfect. You know, no mistakes, no mess-ups. Nothing. Just perfect."

"You know what's funny, Jenny?"

"What?"

"Being humiliated in Muay Thai and then knocking batteries over and stuff?"

"Yeah."

"Well, it makes me think, you know? I think— when I fight, you know, Muay Thai? I think, okay, at least partly I'm fighting humiliation."

"Really?"

"I think so. Sometimes, I think, like, in Muay Thai, they tell you to control your emotions! That's really important. Don't let your opponent know that they're scaring you. Muay Thai's all about control. Controlling your body. Controlling your mind. Controlling your emotions. You know what I mean? And then there's, like, society's conception of women, you know? We're emotional and all that shit! And you know something else?"

"What?"

"I bet there's other girls doing Muay Thai who feel the same way I do."

"Wow, Keira!"

"I know. I know. But let me finish. Just this thing when you knock batteries over? And feel humiliated? Here's what you need to do. Okay, you go into Shoppers to buy batteries. Then you knock the batteries over. Right?"

"Right."

"The cashier comes over, and it's, like, 'Oh, poor blind girl knocked the batteries over.' And then *you*, Jen, you—you say, 'What did I knock over? Batteries? Hey, that's what I came in here to buy. Lucky shot, I guess. I'll take Eveready double-As. If I knocked any of those over, I'll take 'em all."

The seriousness of their conversation evaporated.

"Want another latte, bougie girl...?"

Reliable Witness

"Sorry. Sorry."

Although it was a little startling, her touch, as she put her hand on his forearm, felt soft, almost sensuous. He wondered why she was apologizing, and he wondered whether he had moved into her path or something. Whatever the case, he knew that he should stop. He did, and he made sure that he didn't move his feet. Doing so would change his direction, which would make continuing to walk down the street in a straight line range from very difficult to impossible.

"Hi," Dylan said, turning his look toward the voice. "How are you?"

"Oh, I'm fine. I'm fine," she said.

"Good," he said. He continued looking toward the voice and smiled. The woman sounded a little frantic, he thought, and being friendly, he reasoned, might relax her. Still, he wondered why she had stopped him.

"And you?"

"I'm good. I'm good. Great day, huh?"

As soon as those words came out of Dylan's mouth, he was sorry. *'Great day,'* he chided himself. *Who says that? Nervous people, that's who.*

Man, I'm acting nervous. She sounds a little nervous, and I'm making her more nervous. Man, he continued to chide himself.

"It is a nice day," she said. "It is. I think I'm a little lost. Do you live around here?"

"I do," Dylan said. "Just a little south of the corner up there." He pointed straight ahead.

"So, the ROM...? What is it? The Royal Ontario...?"

"Museum."

"Right. Museum. It's supposed to be around here, but I can't find it. You wouldn't happen to...?"

"Yeah," Dylan said. "I know exactly where it is."

"Oh, good. I've been wandering around for, like, twenty minutes."

"Well, you're not too far away. Maybe a ten-minute walk or so."

"Oh, good."

"Okay. You walk straight down Bloor Street here. You're on Bloor Street."

"Right."

"Just straight down, straight east," Dylan said, concentrating on not moving his feet. "This next street, just up here where the lights are, is Huron. You keep going. The next set of lights is St. George."

"Okay."

"Then you keep walking straight. It's a fairly long block. Then you come to Avenue Road, and there it is! The ROM!"

"Great. Just straight this way, then."

Dylan knew that she was pointing, and he hoped that she was pointing in the right direction—east. She probably was, he concluded.

"Yeah. Straight east. That way," Dylan said, pointing just in case his conclusion was wrong.

"Great," she said. "Thanks a lot. Sorry to bother you. Have a great day."

"No trouble. Enjoy the ROM."

"Okay," she said as she began to walk east on Bloor Street.

"I can't believe it! You actually asked a blind man for directions!" Denise laughed a little.

"I know. I know. It's not funny! I mean, I couldn't believe that I—"

"It's okay, Lisa. It's no biggie," Denise said, putting her hand on Lisa's forearm. "It's really no big deal."

"It *is*. It is. Honest, Denise. I started talking to him, then I saw the white cane. But it was too late. I apologized or something. Oh my God!"

"Okay," Denise said. "Now it's getting really funny."

"No it isn't, Denise."

They were at Gabby's, a café across Bloor Street from the ROM. Lisa didn't go to the ROM as she had intended. Instead, as soon as she met up with Denise in front of the museum, she began to tell her what she had done. It was no good going to the ROM now. She was too upset. Having a coffee was a much better idea. And so there they were at Gabby's.

"You're not gonna believe it," Lisa said.

"What?"

"I was just about to say, you know, 'Where's the ROM'?"

"Yeah."

"And then I saw this white cane! A fucking white cane! I was so embarrassed, so I said I was sorry."

"So what?" Denise said.

"*So what?* Then I touched him on the arm! That's what's 'so what'!"

"You touched him?"

"Yeah. Right on the arm. It was, like, oh, *poor* blind man. It was like I pitied him. I felt awful."

"Well," Denise said, "at least you didn't give him a loonie or something."

"Stop joking around. This is serious."

"Okay, okay, okay." Denise was laughing a little more now.

"Stop laughing. God! You weren't there. I said sorry, and then...then—then you know what I said?"

"What?"

"I said—oh, this is so embarrassing—I said, 'Do you live around here?'"

Denise almost dropped her coffee cup. She put a hand over her mouth. She looked like she was about to spit coffee all over the table, but she managed to swallow it. She then laughed hysterically.

"'Do you live around here?'" she said through her laughter. "'Do you live around here?'"

"I know. Now do you see why I'm so embarrassed?"

"That's hilarious!" Denise said, still laughing. "I can see you now, patting him on the arm. 'There, there, little blind man.... There, there, everything's okay.'"

Lisa began to laugh a little now too. *Still*, she thought, *how embarrassing*. She actually asked a blind man *for directions*. She couldn't believe it!

Dylan made his way to Spadina Avenue and let himself into his apartment. He was still laughing. *Directions...* he thought. *She actually asked me for directions—a blind guy. That's hilarious. Why would anybody do that? We're not the most reliable witnesses around.*

Dylan checked his phone for messages. There were three.

"Hi. It's me. Gimme a call."

It was Joseph. He knew what Joseph wanted. *"Wanna jam at your place Saturday night?"* Dylan got this call in the middle of every week. He played guitar. His friend Joseph also did. Dylan had a piano in his apartment, and another friend played piano. Dylan loved jamming with these guys. He would return Joseph's call later.

"Hello. We are working in your area this week, and we wondered if you would like to have—"

Beep. Deleted. *Damn telemarketing.*

"*Dylan, I'm upstairs working out. It's, uhhh, 2:05. I'll be here for about forty-five minutes or so. If you get this in time, c'mon up. Later.*"

"*End of messages. Main menu.*"

What time is it now? Dylan wondered. He pressed a button on his wristwatch: "*two—oh—nine—p.m.*" He'd just missed Ray's call.

Dylan came out of the kitchen, where he had retrieved his messages. He made his way down the hallway to the bedroom. *Might as well get changed and join Ray upstairs,* he thought. He changed into his Nike track pants and a Nike T-shirt, and before he left his apartment to make his way to the thirteenth floor, he laced up his Nike Airs. He was ready for a workout.

The workout room was small, but it was in his building, and that was a bonus. It had a few pulley machines—bench press, lat pulldown, etc.—and a fairly good selection of free weights. It also had a stationary bike, and Dylan liked this.

"You got my message, eh?"

"Yeah," Dylan said. "How you doing?"

"I'm good. I'm good."

"You're not on the bike, are you?"

"Nope," Ray said. "Hop on. It's all yours. So, what's up man? What've you been doing?"

"Not much," Dylan said. "Just got back from having coffee with Keira."

"Keira! Haven't seen her, like, for....ever. How's she doing?"

"Ah, she's good. She's always good."

"Yeah," Ray said. "You're right about that."

Ray began another set of bench presses, and Dylan, putting his head down, pumped hard on the bike. He sprinted until he heard that Ray was through with his set.

"You wanna hear something weird?" Dylan said.

"You know me, man. I always wanna hear something weird." Ray laughed.

"Okay. Well, check this out. When I was coming home, just now, from seeing Keira, some woman—you're not gonna believe this—some woman asked me for directions."

"What do you mean 'directions'?"

"Directions! She asked me how to get to the ROM!"

"You're kidding. Someone actually asked you...?"

"Yeah. Isn't that weird?"

"Did she know you were blind? Did she see your white stick?"

"Come on, Ray. Of course she did. I mean, I'm walkin' down Bloor Street, right? I got my white stick goin' on in front of me. Of course she saw it. How could she miss it?"

"Well," Ray said, "you must've looked like you knew what you were doing. Otherwise, why ask a blind guy for directions? You musta looked like you knew what was going on."

"I always know what's goin' on, man."

"Yeah. Right. Hey! I betcha she didn't see the white stick. She just wanted to know where the ROM was and didn't notice any white stick."

"I dunno. First thing she said was, 'Sorry.' She said she was sorry."

"For what?"

"I dunno. She just said sorry. And then...and then...you know what she did?"

"What?"

"She touched me...."

"*What?*"

"Yeah. She touched me really nicely, like, kinda sexy, right on the arm."

"Yeah," Ray said. "In your dreams *sexy*."

"Honest, man. It was, like, sensuous. And then...she says to me, 'Do you live around here?'"

"You're kidding." Ray laughed. "'Do you live around here?' Are you serious?"

"I know. I couldn't believe it either. But that's what she said."

"So," Ray said, "she's kind of freaked out.... Then what happened?"

"Nothing. She asked me if I knew where the ROM was, and I told her how to get there, and that was it, off she went to the ROM."

"Ask a blind guy for directions...." Ray was still laughing. "Can't find anybody more reliable than a blind guy."

"Hey, but you know what?" Denise said, interrupting Lisa's thoughts.

"No. What?"

"You got to the ROM. Blind as a bat, he—"

"Don't say that about him," Lisa said. "That's awful."

"Oh. *Sorry*. Didn't mean to offend *your* blind man."

"He's not my blind man, Denise. Just don't say things like that."

"Okay. Okay. All I meant was that—he's blind, right?"

"Yeah."

"So you got to the ROM. He gave you great directions."

"He did," Lisa said. "That's right. Great directions. And he's blind. That's so cool."

"It is cool," Denise said. "I mean, here you are, first time in Toronto, right from Victoria-Hickville...."

"Victoria's a perfectly good city. It's not Hickville."

"Yeah. Right," Denise said. "You're either newlywed or nearly dead. That's it."

"Yeah. Well, kinda. But, still, it's beautiful—ocean, beautiful weather all year round—not like this place."

"Okay. I'll give you that. But...my point is...."

"Your point is what?" Lisa said.

"My point is that you did a real city thing. You asked a blind person for directions."

"That's a city thing?" Lisa said.

"Yeah. It's a city thing."

"How is it a city thing?"

"Like this. You asked a blind guy for directions, right?"

"Okay."

"Well, that's what I mean. I mean, in the city, like, there's actually a blind person—you can actually find a blind person on the street. There's probably no blind people at all in Victoria."

"Yes there is," Lisa said. "Don't be goofy."

"Okay, when's the last time you talked to one? Actually, when's the last time you saw one?"

"Never."

"See? That's what I mean."

"Yeah, but that doesn't mean there's no blind people in Victoria."

"How are we doing here? More coffee? Menu?"

"Oh!" Lisa said. The server had startled her. "I think...uhhh...I dunno. What do you think, Denise? What should we do?"

"Let's have another coffee and go from there."

"Okay," Lisa said.

"So two more cappuccinos?" the server said.

"Yeah," Denise said. "That's great."

With a chipper-sounding "Perfect!" the server left their table.

"Wow," Lisa said. "That guy scared me. I mean, all of a sudden he was right there."

"I know. See, Lisa? Things are quicker here *in the city*."

"Oh, stop it. You loved Victoria when you visited me two years ago. Remember?"

"I know. But here's the thing." Denise leaned toward Lisa and spoke quietly. "I was just visiting; *you* have to live there."

"Okay. I admit it. It's not the liveliest place, not the funnest place. But it's still very beautiful—I mean, sort of relaxing. And as soon as I'm finished my degree...."

"Yeah? As soon as you're finished, then what?"

"Actually," Lisa said slowly, "I was gonna talk to you about this."

"About what?"

"I was gonna talk to you about—well, I'm thinking.... I'm actually thinking, Lisa.... I think I'm gonna move to Toronto when I graduate."

"*Really?*"

"Oh! Sorry!" Lisa said. She had nearly knocked her arm into the server as he arrived at the table.

"No worries," the server said. "There you go. Cappuccinos. Can I get you anything else?"

"I think we're good for now," Denise said.

With a quick "Enjoy!" the server was gone.

"Man," Lisa said, "that guy—that guy...he just suddenly appears. I mean, he's, like, all of a sudden *right there*. I guess that's a city thing too, eh?"

"Nah. The guy's just hyper."

They added some sugar to the cappuccinos and stirred. They looked past one another as they sipped their coffee. A kind of solemnity hung over the table. It was as though the "blind guy" and

Lisa's revelation about moving to Toronto lingered between them, waiting—waiting to be turned this way and that, pulled this way and that, and waiting for some proclamation or, at least, for some conclusion before they drifted away into the vibe that was Toronto.

"You know," Lisa said, breaking the spell of silence, "it really is kinda cool. I mean, blind and still he gave such perfect directions. It's funny. And I like that. I don't know why. Maybe if you're blind...."

"I can see that," Denise said. "If you're walkin' around blind—well, you better...you *better* know where you are."

"I guess that's true," Lisa said. "And if you're like me, and you haven't been to Toronto before, and it's so big compared to Victoria...."

"Told you Victoria was a hick town."

"Don't be ridiculous. I mean that if you're a little scared, like, it's a big city—lots of people, lots of traffic, and you're scared about getting lost or something—then you need someone reliable who can give you directions. Who's more reliable than a *blind person*?"

"That's really, really funny," Denise said. "You need someone who knows what's going on? You need a witness? You need someone reliable? Get yourself a blind guy. You know what I think, Lisa?"

"No. What?"

"I think your blind guy's kinda cool."

"So, you about done?"

"Yeah. Pretty much," Dylan said. "Hold on a sec." He pressed the button on his wristwatch. The computer voice said, *"Three—oh—four—p.m."* "Yeah," he said. "Two more minutes."

"All right," Ray said. "I'm outta here. I'm gonna have a shower. You wanna go for a coffee, beer, or something in a bit?"

"Yeah," Dylan said, pumping the bike hard and breathing just as hard. "Call you when I'm done my shower."

"Okay. Later."

Less than an hour after they had left the gym, Dylan and Ray were sitting on the patio of their neighborhood bar, Kilgour's. They liked the location—right on the corner of Bloor Street and Borden Street—lots of action, lots of people walking along Bloor. For this reason, Ray always sat facing Bloor. Dylan always had his back to it. "That's okay," he had joked once. "I can't see anything anyway. Makes no difference to me which way I'm facing." What Dylan didn't tell him, however, was that he enjoyed Ray's ongoing descriptions of the people walking up and down the street.

"It's like fucking Punk City on Bloor today," Ray said.

"Both of them—skirts right up to their ass," Ray said.

"Okay, the dude is *stoned*," Ray said.

"Jesus, freaks are out," Ray said.

Dylan enjoyed sitting on Kilgour's patio, listening to these play-by-plays. Ray was describing someone now, he realized.

"You'd think..." he was saying. "You'd think—I mean, what is it, 4:15 or so?—I mean, shit, how could she be so wasted so early? She's havin' a short night, that's for sure. Good-lookin' chick, though. Hey, Dylan!"

"What?"

"Go out there. Ask her if she needs directions," he said, laughing and pounding the table with his hand.

"Very funny," Dylan said.

"I still can't believe she asked you for directions. Who'd ask blind a guy? I mean, oh, no offense...."

"None taken, sightie."

"Very funny. I still mean it, though. Asking a blind guy for directions sounds totally weird."

"What do you mean 'weird'?" Dylan said. "It's not weird."

"Come on, man. 'Course it's weird. You're lost; you need directions, right?"

"Right."

"So you look around, aaand, keep in mind, it's a busy street—Bloor Street. Anyway, you look around, and you see people, you know, kinda walkin', strollin' the street, but you don't ask them for directions. Nooo. You spot a blind dude, and you say to yourself, *Now that guy knows his shit. He knows directions.*"

"Exactly," Dylan said. "Exactly. Blind people are focused, man. We need to know where we're at. You sighties...I mean, sometimes you sighties don't have a clue where you are."

"Yeah, yeah," Ray said. "Okay, I'll give you that. But if you know a blind guy, like I do, then maybe, just maybe, you realize that blind guys know where they're at. And then—hang on, hang on," he said, holding off Dylan's interruption. "If you know a certain blind guy, like I know you, then okay. But she didn't know you. For all she knew, *you* were lost and *you* needed directions." Ray was still laughing.

"So you're saying I'm not reliable."

"No," Ray objected. "Sometimes you're reliable. But most of the time...hey, like this. I say, 'Hey, Dylan, see a waitress around?' Then you are *not* reliable at all."

"All right. But I know I'm on a patio and that the waitress will be around soon."

"Right. But you don't see her. I mean, you're not a good witness. You're not reliable. Okay, okay. It's like this...."

"But—"

"No, no. Let me finish. What's that guy's name?"

"What guy?"

"That guy Keira was telling us about—that philosopher guy. You know, the guy. Something like, 'If a tree falls in the bushes and no one's around, does it make a sound?' That guy."

"Oh. I think she was talking about Hume, I think."

"Yeah. Okay. Doesn't matter. But same kinda question."

"What do you mean?

"I mean, like this." Ray assumed a serious comportment. "If a blind guy gives you directions to a place, a certain place...."

"Yeah."

"The blind guy doesn't see that place, never saw it, right?"

"Right."

"Sooo, then...does that place exist?"

"But you know what I think, Lisa?"

"No, Denise. What *do* you think? I can hardly wait to hear."

They both stood, almost simultaneously. They put their jackets on, gathered their stuff from the table, and left the café. They began walking west on Bloor Street.

"What were you saying in there?" Lisa said.

"Oh, right," Denise said. "I think you kinda like this blind guy."

"Don't be ridiculous. I don't even know him."

"I know. I know. But you seemed so embarrassed, you know what I mean? It's like—I know you're embarrassed—but it's, like, you're afraid that you hurt his feelings."

"Well, of course," Lisa said. "Of course I don't

want to hurt his feelings. I mean, he was blind. I don't want to make him feel bad or, even worse, to make him think I'm making fun of him."

"*Fun of him?* How?"

"Come on, Denise. You know what I mean."

"No, I don't."

"Come on," Lisa said, getting a little frustrated. "I go up to a blind man, okay?"

"Okay."

"And I say, 'Hey! What does that sign over there say?' Now that's making fun of someone who's blind. Get it?"

"Yeah. But you didn't ask him to read a sign or anything like that."

"No. But I asked him for directions! I asked a blind man for directions! I mean, how's he supposed to know?"

"Well," Denise said, smiling, "he did know exactly where the ROM was."

"I know. I know."

They walked slowly down Bloor Street, doing their best to navigate the crowds of people. Focused on this task, Lisa and Denise retreated into their own thoughts.

"Are you serious?" Dylan said, laughing. "What do you mean 'does it exist?'"

"Come on, man. Think about it. Like this. If a blind man gives directions to a place he hasn't seen, then okay. Like this. If there's a place, but there's only a blind man around, does that place exist?"

"You're fuckin' crazy, you know that, Ray? You're crazy."

"There's nothing crazy about it. And stop calling me crazy. I don't go around saying you're fucking blind, do I?"

"Well, actually, you do."

"Okay, but I'm right. You are fucking blind," Ray said, laughing.

"And you're fuckin' crazy," Dylan said, laughing too.

"All kidding aside, man," Ray said, "it's pretty funny."

"What is?"

"You know," Ray continued. "It's funny that someone should ask a blind person for directions. I mean, I know we were jokin' around earlier, but there is that thing...."

"What thing?"

"Okay. Like this. If there's something to see, like a place or something, right?"

"Okay."

"Aaand the only person around is a blind guy— I mean, that's the only person around to see it— well, then the blind guy didn't see it, obviously. Thennn does it, does that thing, exist? A blind guy, you know, is not a reliable witness."

"I don't know how you think of this stuff, man," Dylan said.

"Right here! Right here!" Lisa exclaimed. "It was right here!"

"What? What? What are you talking about?" Denise said.

Lisa had stopped walking. She stood very still and looked toward Spadina Avenue; it was about half a block from where she was standing. She had stopped so abruptly that someone had almost bumped into her and had mumbled something— something not so nice—on his way by. Lisa said she was sorry and moved a little closer to the curb.

"It was right here. Right here. This is where I asked him for directions."

"Ooooh," Denise said. "So this is *the* place, is it?"

"Don't be like that," Lisa said.

"Like what?"

"Don't be trolling me."

"I'm not trolling you."

"Yeah," Lisa said, "you are. Just saying; it was right here. Like, right here. I walked up behind him—I mean, like, from behind—and touched his arm, and then said I was sorry. I dunno. Maybe it was the other way around. Maybe I said I was sorry first. I dunno."

"It's okay," Denise said, laughing. "It's okay. Let's keep going. You never know. Maybe we'll run into him."

"Don't be crazy. We're not gonna run into him."

"Okay. Okay. What else do you want to see in Toronto?"

"I dunno. *Your* city. What do you think I should see?"

"The ROM, but—" Denise said, laughing.

"Okay," Lisa said, laughing too. "Some other day. What's next?"

"I know! Honest Ed's, Lisa. You gotta see Honest Ed's. It's closing down soon. You're gonna love it."

"Great," Lisa said. "I think I read about it in the *Globe* or somewhere."

"Yeah. It's a Toronto icon. It's been around, I mean, forever, like, decades. The guy who owns it—I mean, he's dead now—Ed Birvish or Mirbish or something; that's his name. Well, actually, his sons own it now. But when he started it, like, it was a store for people without much money, for people who just moved to Canada. He gave out free turkeys every Christmas!"

"*Really?*"

"Yeah. And the store—it's *real* tacky. At night, there's lights all over it—it's all lit up."

"Wow."

"I know. And it's got all kinds of cheap stuff in it, but it's not, like, you know, stores nowadays, like Walmart and all those; it's just a great affordable store. It's been there for decades, and now—now it's closing."

"Then," Lisa said, "I gotta see it."

They began walking west on Bloor Street toward Honest Ed's.

Moments later, Lisa pulled in close to Denise.

"*I can't believe it! I can't believe it!*" she whispered excitedly.

"What?" Denise said.

"It's him! It's him! Don't look!"

"What are you talking about, Lisa?"

"Let's just cross the street," Lisa said.

"Okay."

"Okay," Lisa said. "Let's just move...just right here. Okay. Don't stare. Okay, see, across the street, on that patio over there?"

"Yeah."

"Well, I think that's him!"

"Who?" Denise said.

"*Him!* The blind guy!"

"You're kidding! Where?"

"On the patio. On the patio."

"Where on the patio? There's all kinds of people on the patio."

"At that table, that table. Don't stare!"

"I'm not," Denise said. "Anyway, what's the difference?"

"Okay. The second table back from the street—see it?"

"Yeah."

"Well, that's him!"

"Which one? There's two guys sitting there."

"The one with the dark glasses. He's wearing dark glasses."

"They're *both* wearing dark glasses," Denise said.

"Louis Vuitton! The one with the Louis Vuittons!"

"I can't see the name from way over here. Don't be.... Is he the one closest to the street or farthest?"

"Closest," Lisa said. "He's sorta got his back to us. That's him!"

"You sure?"

"Oh, yeah," Lisa said. "See? See on the table by his left hand there? Can you see it?"

"Yeah, I see his hand."

"Well, that's his white cane."

"It is? Where? I don't see any white cane."

"No!" Lisa said. "Look. It's folded up. It's all folded up. That's his white cane."

"Oh, right," Denise said. "I see it now. So, that's him?"

"Yes, Denise. Don't stare!"

"Hey, Dylan?"

"Yeah?"

"Okay. Don't stare...."

"What? What're you talking about?"

"All right," Ray said. "Across the street—where Dooney's is?"

"Yeah?"

"Dylan, don't stare!"

"What are you talkin' about?"

"Just look toward me," Ray said. "Don't look across the street."

"Okay. Okay."

"There's a couple of women there."

"So?"

"So…" Ray said, "so…they're looking this way. They're looking at us."

"Yeah? You wish," Dylan said, laughing.

"No. I'm not joking. Honest. They're looking this way. Okay, I'm gonna look at you. I can still see them outta the corner of my eye."

"They're not lookin' at us, Ray."

"What do you know?" Ray said. "Okay, I'm gonna pretend I don't even see them."

"Well, good for you."

"I'm serious, man. They're still lookin' at us. And they're talkin'—like, serious, like real fast."

"Well," Dylan said, "keep your eye on them. Maybe they're assassins out to get us."

"Stop goofin' around. They're lookin' right at us."

"Ignore them," Dylan said. "Maybe they'll go away."

"Yeah, right," Ray said. "I'm gonna go to the can. You good?"

"I'm fine. Thanks, Ray."

"All right. I'm gone."

Dylan sat nursing his pint of beer. He thought about the two women across the street. He wondered whether Ray was right and whether they were looking at them. Ray often exaggerated, but he seemed serious this time. *He actually thinks that the two women across the street are not only looking at us, but talking about us.* Dylan wasn't sure what to make of it.

"Excuse me. Sorry."

The voice startled Dylan a little. It came directly from his right, from off the patio, and it was—*yes*, Dylan thought, *it was*—a woman.

"I'm Lisa. I asked you for directions earlier."

"Oh," Dylan said. "To the ROM? Was that you?"

"Yeah. It was. I'm sorry. I thought you'd recognize my voice."

"Ahhh…" Dylan started to speak.

"Oh my God! I'm so sorry! 'Recognize my voice'—oh, man! I'm so sorry!"

Lisa reached over the patio fence and touched Dylan on the forearm. "I'm sorry," she said.

What They Say

"Excuse me," he said. "I'm just curious. Curious—I'm just curious.... I hope I'm not being obnoxious, but if I'm obnoxious, just tell me to go away."

"Go away," I said.

He laughed and said, "Good call."

I tightened my grip on my partner's arm a little, and she laughed too, although not quite as enthusiastically as he did. I moved my look, in that purposeful way I do, from him to the street. As soon as the light turned in our favour, my partner and I were going across.

"No, no," he said. "I'm just curious. I'm just curious about...like, do you think, like, is it better to see a little bit or just close your eyes and see nothing?"

"I'd like to see a little," I said.

"So...so you don't see anything at all?"

"No."

"Nothing? Zero?"

"Zero."

"Okay, okay." He sounded quite excited now. "Okay, like, what colours do you see?"

"I don't see any colours," I lied.

"None? No colours?"

"None."

He persevered. "Okay. Okay, then, what colours are you imagining?"

Just then I heard a change in the traffic flow. Finally, the light turned in our favour. I moved Hailey's arm forward slightly, letting her know that I'd had enough and we should cross. As we took our first step, I said, "Nothing. No colours. I'm not imagining any colours."

"Okay," he said. "Hey, I'm going the same way you are. Okay, I'll let you go now. Have a good day." He crossed the street quite quickly, it seemed to me—on a bicycle, Hailey told me later.

"Strange again, eh, Bradley?" she said.

"Yeah," I said.

So many thoughts and memories made their way through my mind as she and I walked down the street.

Curious and obnoxious.... One? Both? Is one possible without the other? Can we be one and not the other? Perhaps. But what of curiosity? Is it always obnoxious even when the reverse isn't so? There is at least the fear of coming across as obnoxious, and even as offensive, when curious.

"Sorry. Listen. Sorry," she'd said. "I don't mean to be offensive, and please let me know if I am, but...can I ask...how did you lose your sight?"

"I don't mean to offend you," she'd said. *And...here comes the offense*, I thought. "Like...like, can you see anything or just nothing?"

Blindness is a curious thing, and it is so, at times, even to those of us who are blind. It's also an obnoxious and offensive thing, and it is so, at times, even to those of us who are blind. But what sort of curiosity is blindness? What are we curious about when we are curious about blindness?

It's curious that some people don't see. Blind people don't see, and this makes some people curious. It's curious that even though people see, some don't, some are blind. Most people think that everyone, but for a few, can see, and it's curious that a few can't. Blindness is a curious thing, especially when we approach it or even stumble upon it.

We know people see; more than that, everyone should see. When one of the many things we see is someone who is blind, it makes us curious. What happened? How is it that (you, I) don't see?

"How did you lose your sight?"

"Can you see anything at all?"

"Please don't be offended and let me know if I'm being obnoxious."

"I don't mean to offend you. I'm just curious."

"Something must have happened."

"Is it all dark or all grey?"

"What's it like?"

What happened? Something must have happened. After all, if nothing happened, I would be able to see; I wouldn't be blind. I am blind, you are blind, so something must have happened.

All of this continued to hit me as I walked with Hailey.

"Sorry. Excuse me," he'd said.

"Hi. Me?"

"Yeah. I'm just wondering—just curious. Have you seen an eye doctor? I mean, I'm not trying—I'm not trying to be obnoxious."

"Eye doctor?"

If everyone sees, or, at least, if everyone should see, then someone who doesn't see, doesn't for a reason. There is no reason for seeing. After all, seeing just comes along with birth. We're born. We see. Or, at least, we'll see soon after birth. No reason. We just see. No reason to even think about it. We just see. But blindness—now that needs a reason. Something must have happened. Something must have gone wrong. Something happened to cause you (me) to lose your (my) sight. Something is wrong. You are (I am) blind, and something must have happened to cause it. Nothing causes anyone to see, but something must cause anyone who can't see not to see.

There must be something that can be done about blindness. If the cause can be determined, maybe it can be fixed.

I know it's silly, *he'd probably thought.* He's likely seen an eye doctor. I'm curious. I'll ask him just in case.

"Let your Lord and Saviour Jesus Christ *heal* you, my brother," the man had said. "Let Him return His gift of sight unto you."

"Forward, Smokie. Let's get out of here before I go sighted."

My guide dog, a black Labrador retriever, immediately obeyed my command, and I felt a now-familiar brief hesitation in his movement. He was checking to see if it was safe. And then we were crossing the street.

I thought all these things again later while sitting in my office at the university, a little sad. It wasn't so much what people said about blindness—about me, really—that made me sad.... It was remembering my guide dog, Smokie, that made me sad.

I often thought about him.... He died a few years ago, and...I think of him...often. Sometimes I think of how much joy he brought to me, not only because of the swift and safe way he guided me, but also of the way he embraced my blindness. Working, guiding—that's what blindness meant to him. And...graceful movement...that's what blindness meant to him, and that's what gave me joy, and it even made me feel proud. More than that, though, I loved him, and he loved me and this....

I missed him, and it still hurt. Replace him? Never! Impossible!

I now did what I always did when Smokie's presence flowed into my consciousness and he appeared. I shook my head violently, squeezed my eyes shut, stamped my right foot on the floor, and said, *"No!"* I didn't do this to drive Smokie from my mind. I did it to drive the hard, real world—the world I stomped with my right foot—back in. Smokie would retreat then. He'd curl up in my mind, much in the same way he used to curl up at my feet and rest, and...he'd rest...peacefully and with me.

It's funny, though. It's funny—funny that people, strangers...it's funny.... They just come up to me, ask me things, say things. Sometimes I think my blindness is public property. People aren't trespassing; they're just moving in and out of my blindness as if it were theirs! True, they do apologize, they do say that they're "just curious," that they "don't mean to offend"—they say these things. But then...they move onto my land, my country, the *country of the blind*, as H.G. Wells called it. They're in my country but with only curiosity, not with interest; they're only curious about it—just tourists.

I smiled. I thought, you know, maybe I'll issue passports or even certificates of dual citizenship. Maybe then people could cross the border into the country of the blind for more than curiosity's sake, and maybe...they won't even apologize. *That'd be cool*, I thought, and my smile expanded into a laugh.

It's this white cane, I said to myself as I moved down the two flights of stairs that would lead me to the classroom in which I was about to teach. *It's this white cane!*

When I had Smokie, people asked me about him. They talked about him. They talked about my blindness too, but mostly they talked about him. They didn't even apologize when they did.

They said, "He's so smart."

They said, "He's beautiful."

They said, "Wow! He's fast!"

They said, "I like the way he can tell when the light is green."

They said, "How does he know how to find the address you want to go to?"

They said, "How did he know where the elevator was?"

They said these things and more. I don't know, I thought, maybe they were curious. Maybe they hadn't seen a guide dog working before and were just curious. Maybe...maybe...maybe.... Who knows?

I knew one thing, though: I was happy when they said these things. I knew one more thing: I wasn't happy when they said things now.

I did have to teach soon, and I knew that I had to get going. Heading down those stairs to the classroom took a lot of focus, and I had to start soon.

I didn't like it very much when I got to the classroom just in time. The classroom would be full, and I would walk through the door with my white cane, with all of them looking at me.

Waiting in my office to go down those stairs to teach, that stuff was there in me. It swelled up in me. But, with Smokie, it was different. I loved it then. I loved people looking at Smokie and me as we made our way skillfully and gracefully into the classroom. I loved it no matter where Smokie and I were going. We were a sight to behold. I could feel that.

But, now, that cumbersome white cane. I have that cumbersome white cane. Skill but no grace. There is no artfulness in moving with a white cane. The white cane—the arduous tedium of skill.

I knew I needed to get going, but I couldn't stop thinking about the strange things people say. It's funny. People would say strange things to me while I walked with my partner, Hailey. And they'd say these things to her too.

"Would he like a drink too?" they would say.

"And what will he have?" they would say.

"Sorry for the wait. Here's his health card," they would say.

"Does he want to sit over there?" they would say.

"Does he want us to cut his steak up or can he cut it up himself?" they would say.

"Will he have potatoes?" they would say.

They'd say these things, these strange things, and...they'd say them often. Strange. Very strange.

"You're an angel! You're an angel! You're really an angel!"

"*What?*" says Hailey.

But the woman is gone. She had hurried up Spadina Avenue, moving quickly in the opposite direction from us.

"Who was that, Hailey?" I ask.

"No clue.... I don't know." Hailey turns to look behind her as we continue walking. "Wow! She's almost a block down the street already."

"Well, at least we know you're an angel," I say.

Hailey laughs but in that way of laughing she has that says she is more annoyed than anything else. "I hate when they say that kind of stuff!" she says. "Just 'cause I'm guiding a blind guy, I'm an angel."

"But you are."

"Yeah. She just touched me on the shoulder and said I was an angel. Un*fucking*believable."

We walk in silence for a few minutes. I squeeze Hailey's arm as we walk.

"Strange," she says.

"I know."

"Sorry."

"Thanks, Hailey. Should we have a coffee?"

"Yeah. Good idea.... We have time, right?"

"Yeah."

We stir our coffees without speaking. Hailey breaks the silence.

"You know, I just can't believe it. There's people who still think, ummm, that if you're with a blind guy, well, you're an angel. No one would otherwise be close to someone blind. They think that if you are, you're doing, you know, good work; you're an angel."

"Yeah, I know. Only an angel. What real person would wanna be with someone who's blind?"

"I'm sorry people are so strange."

"Yeah, me too. But remember that time? That other time? It was even worse."

"When?" Hailey says.

"Remember? Remember? We were listening to some Celtic—"

"Oh, right!" Hailey says. "It was the—"

"The Bow and Arrow."

"Right! Right! The Bow and Arrow. Right! Now *she* was strange! I remember she was strange. What did she say again?"

"Well, remember you got up to go to the bathroom?"

"Oh, yeah."

"And then—then when you left.... Remember? I was telling you. She put her hand right on top of mine. I don't know what her partner, or whoever that was sitting with us—I don't know what he was thinking. She just put her hand right on top of mine. And then remember? She said, 'Your friend is so great.' Remember? 'Your friend is so great. She takes you out to listen to music!'"

"Incredible! Isn't it?" says Hailey.

"No kidding. I wanted to say, 'And if I'm *really* good today, she'll take me out again next week.' I didn't say it, but I sure wanted to."

"Yeah, I know. Strange."

Right—around from the banister. The step...the step.... There it is. Okay, now...easy. One, two, three, four, five, six, seven, eight, nine, ten, eleven, down! Okay...turn right...slight angle to the right...right to the door. The mat aaaaand the door. Turn right. Aaaaand the wall. Turn right. First flight. Step...there...okay. Twelve steps, first flight. Banister, banister, banister. Step.... Good. Nine more steps. One, two, three, four, five, six, seven, eight, nine. Straight to the door.

What...what the fuck? Where's the fucking door handle? It's right here.... Where is it?

"Oh, sorry. I didn't mean to touch you."

"It's okay. I was just holding the door open for you."

"Oh...the door's open."

She opened the door. She didn't say a word!

Strange.

Who the hell would do that? How's the blind guy supposed to know the door's open?

There he is—there he is groping for the door handle, the door handle he knows is there. But it's not there! The door isn't there! Did I make a wrong turn?

No, the door is there. I know where I am. Again, strange, but, again, someone must be holding the door open without saying anything!

This seems strange...to me.
This does not seem strange...to them.

"Great!" the facilitator said. "You're all sitting in your chairs, in a circle, all eight of you. Great! Okay, ready?" she continued. "Ready?"

Several murmurs and much nervous laughter came from the eight people in a circle.... In my mind, I called them the Circle of Eight.

Laughter.

"Yeah."

"Mm-hmm."

"Ready as I'll ever be."

"Oh, man."

"Guess so."

"Okay."

"Okay now," the facilitator, Mary, said, "the most important thing for you to know is that you're perfectly safe."

More murmurs and more nervous laughter came from the Circle of Eight.

"You'll be perfectly safe. Actually, this is part of the exercise. *You need to trust!* That's a big part of being blind—trust!"

Several "yeah, right"s and "if you say so"s and "okay"s and "okay ready"s emanated from the Circle of Eight.

Mary spoke again. "Relax. Just relax. That's also a big part of being blind. You need to relax."

Sounds and gestures of feigned relaxation

came from the Circle of Eight.

"Okay. Here we go now. Everyone, okay, put your blindfolds on."

More nervous laughter came from the Circle of Eight, followed by "Jeez…" "Man…" "Shit, I can't see a thing…."

"Okay! Okay, everybody, listen up." Mary's voice grew louder now.

"Listen! Listen! Listen!" Mary's voice was much louder now. "You can't see. You're all blind! What you have left is your hearing. And now, this is so important, you need *to use your hearing.* Use it like you never have before. To do that, you'll have to be still. You'll have to relax. You'll have to be quiet and listen. What do you hear around you? Remember, you're blind now. To know anything, anything at all, you're going to *have to listen!"*

No murmurs. No nervous laughter. The Circle of Eight was quiet. Each of the eight of them had their hands in their laps. Their heads were still. There were no smiles. The Circle of Eight was looking straight ahead.

"Keep listening," Mary continued. "And re-member…'cause memory is very important. Blind people have great memories. And now *you* have to get a great memory too. Try hard to remember what you're hearing. We'll debrief you about this at the end of the activity.

"But now…." Mary's voice became quieter as she took on a more serious tone. "Now…I'm going to give you one more thing to do, but you have to keep listening while you're doing it."

A few murmurs and a little nervous laughter, much quieter than before, came from the Circle of Eight.

"Now...now your touch will come into play. Hearing, memory, and touch. Those are the three *most important things for blind people.* Smell, too, but we'll get to that in a minute."

The murmurs and laughter from the Circle of Eight resumed.

"Okay. Okay, listen. Listen carefully to what I'm saying. Listen. The three most important things to a blind person. Listen, listen, listen."

Laughter and murmurs of agreement came from the Circle of Eight.

"What I'm going to do...." Mary spoke her words more slowly now. "What I'm going to do is pass around an object. The object is not a dangerous one. It won't hurt you."

Sarcastic murmurs of agreement came from the Circle of Eight.

"Seriously. Seriously, the thing won't hurt you. It will fit into your hand. I'm going to give it to one of you. Then I want you to pass it around and then together figure out what the object is. Remember.... It's important to remember that you have to communicate. You have to talk to one another. Who's got the object? Who did I give it to? Which way are you going to pass it around? All these things have to be communicated. And...." Mary spoke very slowly now. "Aaaaand *you are blind now*. This means you can't use your eyes to figure out what the object is or who has it. You need to talk.... That's another thing that's very important to blind people—talking!"

Silently, Mary walked toward one of the Circle of Eight and touched his arm. It made him flinch. "Another lesson," Mary said. "Blind people are used to being touched unexpectedly."

The man laughed and said it was startling, and murmurs and nervous laughter came once again from the Circle of Eight.

Mary asked him to hold out his left hand. He did. She placed an object in it. The object was a hockey puck, but with a twist. It had an electronic device embedded in it, and this device generated a beeping sound from the puck whenever anyone moved it with sufficient force. It didn't take much to trigger the sound, so Mary placed it very gently in the hand of the blindfolded man, and the puck didn't make a sound.

Mary stepped back slowly from the man, who now held the puck in his left hand. The Circle of Eight was silent.

"Okay," Mary said. "Now, in whatever way you can, all of you—each and every one of you—have to somehow examine the object. Then choose a spokesperson. I'll be back in ten minutes, and that spokesperson will tell me what the consensus of the group is. That spokesperson will tell me what the object is. Don't worry. I won't be very far away. I'll be able to see all of you. Everything is still safe.

Do not remove your blindfolds until I tell you to."

Some murmurs of frustration, some of excitement, emanated from the Circle of Eight.

"Oh, right. One more thing. I'm going to take ten steps back. Listen to my voice. Figure out where I am. Whenever you figure out what the object is, let me know, and I'll join the circle. That's your task. You have to figure out how to tell me that you've finished your task." Mary took a few steps backward. She didn't know how many; she didn't count them.

He liked his university office. It had all the stuff, the regular stuff, that made up a professor's office, or so Bradley remembered. He remembered seeing professors' offices when he could see, a little, and he himself had such an office during that time of a little sight. Except for the ever-present computer, how much could have changed? He thought about this now, sitting in his office during the time, this time, when he couldn't see anything at all.

Books were what he loved most of all. Shelves and shelves and shelves up and down the walls of his office—shelves filled with books, shelves of books lining his office walls. This is what he loved.

During that time when he could see a little, Bradley looked at his books. He sat in his office chair and looked at his books. Sometimes he would get up from the chair and move the length of the office walls lined with books. He would touch the books. They were, in some way, his life, or, at least, they represented his life. He admired his books and ran his hand along their spines, caressing them, admiring them, and lamenting. He couldn't see their titles or read their pages, and pages were intended to be read. When he could see a little, magnification technology came between him and his books, and it was technology, and not the books, that brought their words to him. And now even that technology lacked the power to bring his books to him. The separation was complete. He read his books with talking computers. He read them while his books remained in their places on the shelves, unopened.

He let his eyes roam to where he knew his books were, resting on shelves. He sat in his office chair, looking at his books in a way that, had anyone seen him, they would have described as contemplative. Contemplating was not what he was doing though.

I should never have agreed to this meeting, he thought. *Damn. Oh well. I'll just tell her no and that's that. Why the hell didn't I tell her this when she phoned yesterday?*

"Knock, knock. Hi, Bradley." She said this cheerfully as she pushed the almost closed door of his office fully open and walked in.

"Hey, Mary. Come on in. Come on in. Have a seat."

Mary sat. Her eyes were immediately drawn to

the shelves of books. There were a lot of them. She looked at them curiously and then snapped her eyes away from them.

"So, what did you think of that session yesterday?" she said.

"Yeah. It was okay. Okay."

"It was good you were there," Mary said. "See, like, well, it was good you were there, 'cause, well, you were only there for the blind piece, but you got a sense of what we're trying to do."

"Right. Yeah."

"It was good you were there, kinda off to the side, kinda sorta observing. Oh, you know what I mean."

They both laughed a little. Bradley sensed Mary was nervous in the way she laughed.

"Well, now that you've observed one of our pilots," Mary continued, "at least the blind piece, you have a better idea of what we want to do. We're going to roll this out all across the university starting next month." The greetings, the friendly chat, were now over. It was now time to speak earnestly.

"Mm-hmm."

"The last Thursday of every month—that's when we're going to roll this out. We're all very excited! At the end of the day, the university finally realized they needed disability awareness training moving forward. Aaaand this is where you, Bradley, come in. We would love to have you on board! Success! Success! Achievement! This is our motto. Not disability. But ability! People with disabilities are, at the end of the day, people—people just like you and me. Well, you know what I mean."

"Yeah," Bradley said, laughing. "We're people, just like you."

"I know. I know. Sorry. But you know what I mean." Mary laughed nervously and continued. "I mean...I mean, having a person with a disability— I mean, a *real* blind person—and this is great, I mean, 'cause you're *totally* blind! And you were *there*, showing these folks that you have ability—not disability but ability!"

Mary's voice not only raised an octave but also sped up. "To have a successful professor, a blind successful professor, a blind professor who teaches and who writes books"—her eyes flashed back to the shelves of books for a moment—"this makes our training sessions very, very viable. And...*believable!*"

"Sooo," Bradley said, "you want me there— there at these training sessions—as a demo?"

"No, no. You'd be there as an *example*, as *proof* that people with disabilities *have* abilities. You know, we need to show these folks the abled disabled. Oh, and plus we'll do the practical piece. You know, the piece that shows the folks what it's like to be disabled, and you—you can talk about how you *overcame* your disability. And then you can give them some theory. You know, the disability studies approach. This way we get all our bases covered. We'll give folks a training piece that is consistent and coherent aaaaand, especially, *believable!*"

"Really?" Bradley said.

"Yes. Our action plan, and now this third successful pilot, shows the university they have to come on board with disability awareness training. Really. The train has left the station, and folks have to get on board or get left behind!"

Bradley sat looking at his books once more, listening...and not. He had, of course, heard this kind of talk and these kinds of expressions before, and they never failed to intrigue him. "Moving forward." "Trains leaving stations." He thought these things as he listened, looking at his books.

She actually believes what she's saying. She has no idea. I really can't handle much more of this do-gooder social justice bullshit.

Bradley was most intrigued and most annoyed with this "overcoming" talk. *Overcoming my disability?* he thought. *It's too phony. Overcoming myself, that's where it always leads. Man, I'd like to tell her I can't overcome anymore. I need to be my disability. I need to live it.*

Bradley thought these things as he listened to Mary and looked at his books. *How can I tell her these things?* he wondered.

"So," Mary said, "we think it would be wonderful if you would come on board and join the team. It would give sooo much credibility to our project."

Mary left his office disappointed, Bradley knew. Still, she left as cheery as ever.

"Well," she'd said, "thanks, and I'll let you know how things play out. Do you want your door shut?"

"No, you can leave it open. Thanks."

When Mary was gone, Bradley continued to sit, looking at his books. He then slowly stood. He took his bag from his desk and hung it over his shoulder. Time to teach. He turned and moved toward the door, to where his white cane stood leaning to the right of the door jam. As he drew closer, he reached out with his right hand to where he knew his cane would be....

Right in the forehead!

Mary had left the door open...halfway.

For Her

For her. For her.

These words raced through Jenny's thoughts as she went over the events of last night.

For her.

She couldn't believe that the server had actually said that. She couldn't believe, either, that no one said anything. *Disgusting*, she thought.

She cranked up the tension on her stationary bike and began to shed her anger. The server had said, "For her?" and *that* got her pissed. But she was also angry that no one—including her—no one said anything. She wasn't sure which one of these things made her angrier.

Forty-five minutes later, Jenny sat on the couch in her apartment on Huron Street in Toronto's Annex, drinking coffee. She had pounded her bike for twenty minutes and had a shower, turning the hot water all but off for the last few minutes. Despite this, she was still angry.

Stuff like this happened to Jenny more often than she liked. And, more often than not, it didn't get her angry, at least not as angry as she'd gotten last night. It was the server, and yet many servers said similar things. "What does she want?" "What will she have?" This was common enough. Jenny heard this all the time, or so it seemed. *Why last night? What was it about last night?*

They came up from the Spadina subway station and made their way to Bloor Street. They stopped on the corner of Bloor Street and Spadina Avenue. This corner represented a crossroads for them, since one of them lived in one direction and the other in the opposite one. They stopped on the corner now, wondering whether they should go their separate ways.

"What do you wanna do?" Keira said.

"I dunno," Jenny said. "You?"

"I dunno. Uhhh, what time is it?"

Jenny pushed a button on her wristwatch. "*Ten—thirty-three—p.m.*," its computer voice said. "It's, like, ten-thirty," she said.

"Still early," Keira said. "Wanna grab a coffee, drink, or something?"

"Yeah. It's still early. Glass of wine, maybe. Man, now that I think about it, I could use a glass of wine."

"You like this place?" Jenny said.

"Yeah. It's all right. What's wrong with it?"

"Well, kinda *bougie*, isn't it? Even for you," Jenny teased.

"What do you mean 'even for me'?" Keira said.

"I *mean* even for *you*. You're bougie, but not *this* bougie."

"Yeah," Keira said. "That's me. Bougie Keira. So, what do you want to drink?"

"I guess they have wine here. Right?"

"Of course. This is a bougie place. Of course they would have wine."

Jenny laughed and said, "How much is a glass of red? Like, ninety-three dollars?"

"If you want the cheap house red," Keira said, laughing too. "Okay. Okay," she whispered. "Here comes the guy. Let's just get two glasses of Malbec, okay?"

"Yeah. Okay."

"How are you this evening?" The server placed two bar serviettes on the low table between them. "Drinks for you?"

"Yes," Keira said. "Do you have Malbec? I mean, by the glass?"

"We do. We have a really nice Malbec from Argentina. A couple of glasses?"

"Yes, please," Jenny said.

"You've got it. Oh, having something to eat tonight? Or just drinks?"

"Just booze," Jenny said, laughing.

"I know what you mean," the server laughed. "Be right back with your booze."

Jenny felt the arm of the couch she was sitting on. *Nice soft leather*, she thought. *Thick carpeting, too*. This was her first time in this bar. *'Proof,'* she thought. *What an odd name for a bar*. She thought this might have something to do with whisky—proof, some sort of percentage—that's how they sometimes talked about whisky, didn't they? *Oh, well*, she thought. *It's a hotel bar—the InterContinental Hotel, no less—so...what do you expect? Proof...? That's okay.*

"This table sure is low," Jenny said.

"Yeah. I kinda like it."

"Yeah. Me too."

Jenny rubbed her hand on the surface of the table. It felt like glass. *Maybe it is*, she thought. *Smooth couches, smooth tables, thick carpeting—quite the place.*

"Keira?"

"Mm-hmm?"

"Doesn't sound like too many people in here. Is there?"

"Uhhh...." Keira turned in her seat, looked over one shoulder, then the other. "Not too many. I'd say...about.... Let's see. There's a couple tables of four, two with three, and, I think, one, two...there's five people at the bar."

Jenny folded her white cane and placed it on the table in front of her. She had held it, unfolded, in her left hand until the server had taken their order. This was enough, she thought. Enough for the server to notice it and figure out that she was blind. *You'd think*. Jenny laughed.

"What's so funny, Jen?" Keira asked.

"Nothing, really. I was just thinking about that server earlier, at that other place."

"Oh, yeah. That was horrible."

"I couldn't believe it," Jenny said. "'For her'! 'For her'! I couldn't believe she actually said that.... I mean...."

"I know what you mean. 'Sooooo, you'll have the shrimp, annnnnd...for *her*?' 'For her'! She was asking *me* what *you* wanted to order!"

"I know, Keira. But that's not the first time that's happened."

"I know. But still.... 'For her'! I think it was the way she said it; I think that's what bugged me. You know, '*For herrr.*' It was so condescending."

"Yeah. I think so. I think that's what bugged me too. It made me so mad."

Why was this making her so angry? *Stuff like this happens all the time, so why did it make me so angry this time?* There was nothing different about last night.

She sat on her couch, sipped her coffee, and tried to remember what she was up to today. *One o'clock*, she recalled. *Nothing until one o'clock.* That meeting would be difficult, she knew. Breaking in a new reader always was. They had their ideas about how to read to blind people, and it was hard sometimes to change their minds. *Funny*, she thought. *Once someone gets some knowledge about blindness they become an expert. They suddenly know better than you about what blind people need. They know better than I do about what I need.* Jenny laughed at this and took another sip of her coffee. *That's funny*, she thought. *Really funny.*

Jenny was glad that she got twenty minutes in on her bike. She had been so busy last week. Twice. Was it only two times? Twice. That's right. Twice. That was it. Only twice on her bike. Well, the twenty minutes this morning made up for it. She'd really pushed it.

For her.

What was that about? Jenny wondered. There were other times, too, many of them, where people did the same thing, or a similar thing. She recalled the time when she went to that play. What was it...? Oh, right, *Hair*. She went to *Hair* with Phil. That's right. It was Phil. The same thing happened, she remembered.

"Is she with you? Are you guys together?" the usher had asked.

"I *am* with him. We *are* together."

Jenny laughed a little as she remembered.

She remembered how aggressive she had been, and how she answered the usher's questions in the theatre before Phil had a chance.

She remembered how embarrassed the usher was. "Well, I didn't mean—sorry. Sorry, I didn't mean...."

She remembered how she reached out toward him as though to touch him to tell him that it was okay.

She remembered laughing and asking him,

"Where did you say our seats were?"

She remembered talking with Phil, laughing, before the curtain went up.

And she remembered, too, brushing tears from her cheeks while the audience quieted and the curtain rose.

"Made *you* so mad?" Keira said. "It made *me* really mad! But I know what you mean. Of course you were mad."

"I was," Jenny said. "But, Keira, you know what?"

"What?"

"Well.... Well, what I can't," Jenny continued slowly, "figure out—I mean, for the life of me—what I can't figure out is why I got so mad."

"Why you got so mad? Come on, Jen, you had every right to be mad. She was so condescending, so patronizing."

"I know. I know. She was. But still...it's not such a big deal...."

"Not such a big deal?"

"It's not such a big deal. 'For her?' 'What's she gonna have?' Lots of people ask that."

"All right, ladies, here's your drinks. For you. And yours is right in front of you."

Jenny and Keira said their thanks.

"Just let me know if there's anything else you need—menu, food...."

"We will," Keira said.

"Enjoy."

"Is he gone?" Jenny whispered.

"Yeah. But if he wasn't, he woulda heard you."

They both began laughing. Jenny lifted her glass of wine and gestured toward Keira. They said, "Cheers," and sipped.

"See? Now that was okay," Jenny said.

"What? The wine?"

"No. I mean what the guy said, the waiter—*that* was okay."

"You mean 'enjoy'? You mean when he said 'enjoy'?"

"Stop messing around, Keira," Jenny said, laughing. "You know what I mean. 'Here's your wine. It's in front of you.' I mean when he said *that*."

"Oh *that*," Keira said, laughing too. "That. Yeah. That was pretty cool—not like that chick earlier."

"Yeah. No kidding."

"I can't figure it out, Jen. I mean, I don't know why, like—I don't know why they all don't do that."

"Yeah. They can see my stick, for God's sake."

"That's for sure. I mean, what was she *thinking* back there? What was she...? What was her name? Bre...?"

"Brenda."

"Yeah, Brenda," Keira continued. "What was she thinking? You had your glass of wine. Actually, you had *two*. She brought you two glasses of wine. She could see your white stick."

"I know. Plus, I came in—I came in the damn place with it. And then when we were sitting, I didn't fold it up. I held it. I held it. I figure...I think, well, here I am. I walk in with a white stick. I sit down with a friend. We're at a table. I'm holding my white stick out. I mean, you'd think the whole damn place could see it. You'd think, if she's got working eyeballs, that chick should know I'm blind."

"No kidding."

"I'm not gonna go back there, I dunno, for a long time."

"Forever," Keira said.

"Yeah," Jenny said. "Forever. That'll teach her."

As though it were scripted, Jenny and Keira both laughed and, through their laughter, mocked the server. "That'll teach her!" The phrase became a chorus for their laughter.

Jenny had heard it first; she was recalling it now. She remembered poking Chantelle in the arm. "Pre-boarding. It's pre-boarding. Let's go."

"Okay. Okay. Don't poke me so hard."

They stood. Jenny unfolded her white cane and took Chantelle's arm, and they began making their way to the counter for pre-boarding.

"Imagine," Chantelle said. "Four and a half, five hours, and we're in Vancouver."

"I know. I'm thrilled to get out of Toronto for a

while. Everything's so nice and fresh in Vancouver."

"Yeah. I'm thrilled that the conference is there this year."

There wasn't much of a lineup for pre-boarding, and Jenny and Chantelle were soon showing their boarding passes and ID.

"Thanks. On your way to Vancouver?" the Air Canada representative said as he examined their passes.

"Sure are," Jenny said.

"Wait! Wait! You guys—you guys travelling together?"

"Yes. We are," Chantelle said.

"Okay. But you're in different seats. I mean—I mean, you're not sitting next to each other! This isn't any good! Why aren't you sitting next to each other?"

"I dunno," Jenny said. "We didn't arrange the seating."

"No!" The rep became flustered and very anxious. "No," he repeated. "You need to be sitting together."

"Why?" Chantelle said.

"Why?" he said. "Why? Well, 'cause...'cause she's blind!"

"Well, *there's* a good reason," Jenny said, laughing. "It's really okay. Really. We'll manage."

"No! It's just...it's just...." The rep was getting more and more flustered. "It's just—I mean, if you're travelling together, you should be sitting together."

"Makes sense," Chantelle said.

Jenny was still laughing a little and trying her best to make light of the situation. *And*, she thought, *calm this jerk down.*

"No, no. Okay, I'm gonna have to change this. I'm gonna have to change your tickets. I mean, I'm gonna have to change your boarding passes. You've got to sit together. Okay, step over here. Just wait here. I'm going on board, and I'm gonna change things. There's got to be a better way." He turned to his coworker. "Maxine, I'm headed on board. Just get someone to look after pre-boarding for a minute."

Jenny and Chantelle stood where the Air Canada rep had asked them to. Neither of them liked the fuss being made over them. They were getting a lot of attention, and this kind of attention they could do without.

"What's wrong with the guy?" Chantelle said.

"I dunno. He's freakin' out. He doesn't want me travelling alone."

"I guess not," Chantelle said.

"No. Can't let the blind girl sit on a plane by herself."

"Weird."

"Yeah, well," Jenny said, "that's what it's like. Don't let the blind girl travel alone. You're gonna have to help her out. Take her to the bathroom. Do a special safety thingie—you know, a demo. Bring her a drink. Show her where it is. Blah, blah, blah. *Way* too much trouble."

"Is that it?" Chantelle said.

"Come on, Chantelle. You've been around. That's exactly what it is. You know that. Get someone else to help the blind girl, then you don't have to. But you know what? I don't even blame them. They're way too busy on planes nowadays. They don't need some blind chick making it hard for them."

"I guess not...."

"But still," Jenny said. "Still."

"Yeah."

"Hey!" Jenny said. "Let's cheer up! Maybe they'll move us into first class."

"Yeah, right," Chantelle said.

"Okay. All taken care of." The Air Canada rep was back. "It's all good. You guys are moved right up into business class. You're sitting together. Now," he said, looking at Jenny, "your friend can look after you."

"Thanks," Chantelle said.

"First. Class." Jenny whispered these words to herself.

"Oh, and you know what else is *really* hilarious, Jen?"

"What?"

"Okay, listen to this. The server, uh, what's her name, Bru...?"

"Brenda. Brenda."

"Yeah. Brenda. Okay, listen to this. She's *goth!*"

"She's what?"

"Goth! You know, *goth*!"

"Oh, goth. What do they look like?"

"Kinda, like, *dark*," Keira said.

"Dark?"

"Yeah. Their *mood*. They try to give off this mood, you know, *dark*—a dark mood, like a dark vibe."

"How do they do that?"

"Okay. First, the hair. The hair is dark."

"You mean they dye their hair black?"

"Sometimes. But this chick—she already had black hair."

"Oh."

"So she tied it back, and it looked *severe*, like, that her face is really white and her lips are dark purp—"

"Is she white, Keira?"

"Yeah. Yeah. She's white."

"Are there any black people? I mean, any black goths?"

"Good question. I don't know. There has to be. But you know what? I'm thinking this goth thing—I'm thinking it's, like, a white thing."

"Yeah. Probably. That we gotta find out."

"Yeah. We will. So...."

"Okay," Jenny said. "So Brenda's got a really white face, really white, but she's dark. What kind of lips?"

"Dark purple! She had dark purple lipstick."

"So really dark lips on a really white face? Scary?"

"Kinda."

"And, I guess, dark eye makeup too?"

"Yeah. Yeah."

"Man. So, Keira, what was she wearing?"

"But, well, obviously black."

"Okay. I know, but, like, *what* was she wearing? Like, jeans? Like what?"

"Jeans," Keira said. "Tight black jeans. And the compulsory combat boots. Not the ones with the big platform soles, you know, 'cause she was working at the bar. Just regular—regular combat boots."

"What about her top?" Jenny said.

"Right. A tank top, a *Joy Division* tank top."

"The band?"

"Yeah."

"Joy Division?" Jenny said. "It's a goth band?"

"It is. Yeah."

"Wow! I didn't know that."

"Yeah," Keira continued. "And then the black tank top—it had white figures. I don't mean *figures* exactly—like, white *lines* on the black background."

"What do you mean?"

"Well, kinda like lines, like mountain ranges. I mean, like, topographical."

"I don't get it."

"Okay, Jen. Black tank top...."

"Yeah."

"...with white lines...."

"Yeah."

"Like, repetitive mountain ranges."

"Repetitive? What's that supposed to mean?"

"It's topography. Topography. You must get that—topography!"

"No. I don't get it, Keira."

"Okay. Well, forget it. I can't explain it any better than that. What do you think I am, audio description?"

"Okay. Okay." Jenny began laughing and Keira joined in.

"Okay, what else?" Jenny continued. "I mean, like, jewelry? Tattoos?"

"Oh, right! That's the coolest thing, Jen."

"What?"

"The pentacle."

"The what?"

"Pentacle. Pentacle. You know, the five-pointed star enclosed in a circle."

"Oh, like a pentagon."

"Right. Right. And each of the points touches the circumference of the circle."

"Where was that?" Jenny said.

"She had it. Like, with a lotta goths, it's like a ring, a pentacle ring. But...."

"Brenda was wearing a ring? A pentacle ring?"

"No! That's the super cool thing. It was a tattoo!"

"A tattoo! Where?"

"That's the cool thing. A tattoo on her *finger*!"

"Wow!"

"Yeah. She had a pentacle ring tattooed on her finger."

"Which finger? Which hand?"

"Her right, I think. I can't remember."

"That is cool," Jenny said. "A ring tattooed right on your finger."

"I know. And you know what else? This is really, really cool—*really* gothlike."

"What?"

"A chain. I mean a...."

"A chain? What kind of chain?"

"A little, thin chain. But she had a nose piercing."

"Yeah?"

"And from that, from her nose piercing, was a chain. The chain goes from *that* piercing to an ear piercing. That's really goth."

"Wow!"

Leaning back on the leather couch, Jenny sipped her wine and tried to picture (at least she tried to do what she thought people did when they pictured things) this goth look. Dark. Combat boots. Black. Piercings. It was difficult for her to picture.

"So," Keira said, "that's the goth server, Jen. That's what she looked like. Top it all off with that black polish on her fingernails and...you got goth."

"Yeah," Jenny said. "You got goth, all right. And the voice, Keira.... Man."

"You mean the robotic voice? No intonation, no expression? That voice?"

"Yeah," Jenny said. "It's, like, when she speaks—I mean, I have a picture of her face."

"Really?"

"Really. I have this picture. You know, no facial expression, no smile, nothing. Is that right?"

"Right on," Keira said. "You are dead on."

"I guess, I mean, like, the goth—I guess they're trying to give this, you know, 'I don't give a shit' thing."

"Exactly," Keira said. "Exactly. It's, like, meaninglessness. Life has no meaning. You're supposed to look, well, blank. Like you just don't care. Life is meaningless and so you don't care."

"I get it. That's funny, but I get it."

"I know," Keira continued. "They read all this stuff, all this stuff about the meaninglessness of life."

"Like who? You mean those existential writers?"

"Yeah. They read Franz Kafka, Friedrich Nietzsche...you know."

"Okay. But, you know, I read those people too, Keira."

"I know. But they wanna be real heavy. 'Life is real heavy; I'm beyond all of that.' You know."

"Yeah."

"That's damn ironic, ain't it, Jen?"

"How so?"

"Well, okay, like this. She's a goth, right?"

"Right."

"So she's beyond all the trivial things of life. She's past all this meaningless stuff that all the other people are into. Beyond all of that. She's on a different plane."

"Okay."

"But then," Keira continued, "then a blind person walks into her bar. She doesn't have a clue. She doesn't know what to do. She freaks out. Can't even talk to the blind woman. 'For her'! 'For her'! She has to talk to the sighted chick. The blind woman's got her freaked out."

"I get it," Jenny said, laughing.

"I know, right?" Keira joined Jenny in her laughter. "It's so ironic! I mean, the goth just gave a whole bunch of meaning to blindness, all of it negative!"

"That's real goth, eh?"

"Sure is."

There was that time on Queen Street West, Jenny was remembering, that time at that new restaurant, the one she hadn't been to before.

"I like this patio," she remembered saying to Lisa.

"I know. Me too. It's big enough so you can sit far enough from the street that you don't hear all the noise. But you're still close enough to see everything—you know, all the people."

"That's great. Since you're facing it, let me know, like, if there's anything interesting going on."

"I will," Lisa said. "That's why I sat facing the street. I looove watching the people on Queen Street."

They were just coming from a play, just down the street, in the park—Trinity Bellwoods Park. She really liked the play, *Zong!* It was incredible, she thought. The author, the actual woman who wrote it, was there and in the play. NourbeSe Philip was actually in the play. Jenny loved that.

"So, you...?" A male voice at their table.

"It's okay," Lisa said. "It's okay. One will do."

Jenny heard a thump on the table. It sounded as though someone had dropped something on it. Then she heard the man say, "Your server will be out in a minute."

"What was that, Lisa?"

"The guy. The maître d', I guess. It was weird."

"Whaddaya mean?"

"Well, he looked at you and then at me. He was holding two menus up toward me. I said it was okay; we'd just need one."

"Yeah," Jenny said. "I heard that."

"Right. And then he just dropped them. I mean, he just dropped both menus on the table. It was real quick. Then he said, 'Your server will be right out,' and then he almost ran back inside."

"Wow!" Jenny said. "That is weird."

"Yeah. It was like he got scared."

"Yeah."

"I mean, weird. It was like...like he was scared of you!"

"Probably. That's me. Scary Jenny. You never know.... You never know.... I could hurt them. They could catch blindness from me."

They both laughed. And yet there was something in their laughter that didn't find the situation funny.

Their server was good. She said her name was Jackie and that she would be their server all evening. Jenny didn't seem to scare her. Jenny left her white cane unfolded anyway. She leaned it against the table—in plain sight, she told Lisa. Lisa thought that it was a good idea and that it was good that her cane was there "for anyone to see," as she put it. They ordered their meals without incident.

"There you go. Seafood linguine for you, and...the pasta special for you."

Jenny and Lisa thanked Jackie. Lisa said that her meal looked great. Jenny laughed and said that hers smelled great. All three laughed, and with a cheerful, "Enjoy!" Jackie was gone.

"It really does smell good, Lisa."

"Yeah. Sure does. And yours looks good, too."

"Great."

At least the server was okay, Jenny thought. *What was her name? Jackie, right? Jackie. She was okay.* She wasn't *great* but neither were Jenny's expectations, so okay, well, that was good enough. Blind people shouldn't expect too much, she thought as she smiled. *Satisfactory*, she thought. *Yes, satisfactory—that's good enough for us blinks.*

"Fresh ground pepper?"

These words brought Jenny out of her musings. Across the table, standing next to Lisa. She could tell by his voice. He was asking Lisa whether she wanted pepper—freshly ground, no less—on her meal. What he said next, though, made Jenny blink.

"Does she want some pepper?"

He just asked Lisa. He asked Lisa! Not me, Jenny thought. *Lisa—he asked Lisa!*

"Jenny?" Lisa said.

"Yes?"

"The man here wants to know if you want freshly ground pepper on your meal."

"Tell him no thanks, Lisa."

"My friend says that it's okay; she doesn't want any pepper."

Lisa laughed. She tapped Jenny on the hand and said, "Can you believe it? He's gone."

"He actually asked you.... He asked you, Lisa—you. 'Does she want pepper?'"

"I know," Lisa said. "It's pathetic. I'm sorry. I'm really sorry."

"Not your fault," Jenny said, withdrawing her hand from Lisa's touch and locating her napkin. "Not your fault."

"Still...."

"What do you think? Another glass?" The server was back.

Jenny sat up straight on the leather couch. She located her glass on the smooth low table. "Oh, man," she said. "It feels empty."

"It sure is," the server said. "Another?"

"What do you think, Keira? One more and then go?"

"Yeah. Why not? I'm empty too."

"Any food? The kitchen's closing in about fifteen minutes, so last chance for food."

"No. I'm okay. What about you, Jen?"

"I'm fine. I'm fine. Just booze."

"You got it. That's my kinda meal. Just booze. Right back with your Malbec."

"Kitchen's closing?" Keira said. "What time is it, anyway?"

"*Eleven—eleven—p.m.*," Jenny's watch told her. "About ten after eleven," she said.

"Ah. That's not too bad. I thought that, uh, you know—I thought it was, like, midnight or something."

"No," Jenny said. "Still early."

"Here you go. There. And...there's yours. Got your old glass, and your fresh glass is right where the old one was."

"Thanks so much," Jenny said.

"No prob. Enjoy."

"Now," Jenny said, "he's a *great* server!"

"Thanks, Keira. You didn't have to pay. But thanks."

"After what you went through earlier tonight? That's the least that could happen to you—a couple of glasses of wine. My pleasure."

"Well, thanks again."

"Okay," Keira said. "This way...around...oh. What do you think? Bathroom before we go?"

"Yeah. Good idea."

"'Scuse us. Coming right behind you."

"Oh, sorry!" a woman said. "Sorry."

"No. It's okay," Jenny said. "We're good."

"You know..." the woman spoke again. "You know, I saw the two of you come in, and you looked like you were having a good time. You were laughing. You seemed happy and—"

"It was the wine," Jenny said, laughing. "I really don't like her."

"Yeah," Keira said, laughing too. "It was the wine."

"Oh, you two," the woman said. "I can tell. You're best of friends."

"True," Jenny said.

"And you're so good to her," the woman said, looking at Keira. "It's nice to see them get out."

"Yeah," Keira said sharply. "I'm takin' her right back to the home. Let's go, Jen."

"Yeah," Jenny said. "Let's get outta here."

The View

"This is an amazing view!" They all say it.

"What a view!" they say. "This is awesome!" they say. "You've got a great view!" they say. "This is amazing! You can see all of downtown Toronto!" they say.

He had heard this about the view many times. He even said it himself. "Amazing view, isn't it?" he would say to his friends. But he was joking and they knew he was.

They would laugh and he would laugh. What he said *was* funny, but there was something more than humour in their laughter.

It was true; he did have an amazing view from the balcony of his apartment. You could see all of downtown and the lake, Lake Ontario, from the eighth-floor vantage point of his balcony.

You could see *the view*—but only if you could see. And he couldn't. He was blind.

Sitting in the bar in the Sylvia Hotel in Vancouver, Bradley and Hailey, along with their friend Adam, were talking about being blind as they often did when they got together. They didn't get together very often, once a year or so. Bradley and Hailey lived in Toronto, and Adam lived in San Francisco. They were good friends despite the distance that separated them.

Their work was what brought them together...and their friendship grew.

Bradley and Hailey were professors at the University of Toronto. They did their scholarly work in the field of what the academy has come to call disability studies. Adam was a playwright, a poet, and an actor. Many of his plays and much of his poetry held the theme of disability, particularly blindness. Adam, too, was blind. This work, this blindness—this is what brought the three of them together.

"Two totally blind guys, completely blind, in the same place, in a bar. That's rare. You guys are rare. Two in the same place. That's funny."

"That's true, Hailey," Bradley said.

Laughing, Adam said, "That is rare. But what's really funny is that guys like me and you, like me and you, we're called total...totally blind."

"I like to say 'completely blind,'" Hailey said.

"I know. Everybody says that," Bradley said.

"Yeah," Adam said, "but...but what's funny— so, what's funny—it's funny that people who can hardly hear anything or who are totally deaf—we call them 'profoundly deaf.'"

"Yeah, exactly...exactly. How is it that they're called 'profound' and we're not, Adam?"

"Yeah, man, we're cool...we cool. We profound!"

Adam's style of speaking was becoming more pronounced and just as profound as total blindness. He didn't have an accent. Adam insisted on this. He was African-American with Mississippian roots. His people were from Mississippi, he'd told them. "But I were born and raised in California. I now talk street talk."

Hailey looked at them. Two profoundly blind guys—one white, one black.

She thought about this as she watched them. She thought of those times the three of them walked down the street together, went into a restaurant, into a bar just like this one. She thought of them, one white man, one black man, both blind, and...one white woman who could see. She thought mostly of the looks—the looks people gave them, looks that made her feel uncomfortable. They were also looks of curiosity, and sometimes people even smiled. But there were looks. There were looks, and there were looks as they walked into this bar earlier this evening too.

Hailey wondered about these looks. She remembered the three of them walking into a café in Toronto awhile back—the three of them, Bradley holding her right arm, and Adam taller than the two of them with his hand on her left shoulder. As they moved through the door, she remembered, people looked, their forks suspended in mid-air; they were silent...looking.

She remembered the looks, so many looks. All the looks. Looks looking at the likes of them.

"We definitely, with no question, we profound, we profoundly blind!" Adam continued.

All three of them enjoyed Adam's proclamation. They all continued laughing.

Bradley and Adam did a high-five and a fist bump in celebrating their new "profound" status. They took pride in high-fiving and fist-bumping each other.

"This shit is no easy task for a couple of profoundly blind dudes," Bradley said.

"Sure ain't," Adam said. "But we cool, we profound. We got it. We wit' it."

"You guys are cool," Hailey said. "But...but...I'm profoundly blonde."

"Yeah. And...you, Bradley..." Adam said, "you drink that light beer shit. He profoundly Wonder Bread."

They laughed, and this time they all did a fist bump.

"Right!" Hailey said. "Actually, you two, the two of you, it's not...it's not that you're totally blind, like, sightless, you know what I mean?"

"Yeah," Bradley and Adam agreed.

"Profoundly blind says that you two have some sort of sight. It's not that you're sightless. I mean, you don't have strict physical or biological sight, but you have some kind of sight."

"Right! You've got something there," Bradley said.

"Y'all got somethin' profound emergin'," Adam added.

Hailey's eyes opened very wide. Adam and Bradley could tell. "You know what it is? This is it. This is it. You two have a view!"

They both laughed at her.

She saw that they were tilting their heads at angles that gave them a quizzical look. *Looking at each other? Could they be looking at each other? Could they?* It sure looked like it.

She knew, from living with Bradley and from knowing other blind people such as Adam, that they typically looked toward the voice of those with whom they were speaking. She knew this and she knew that they did this partly out of habit. And she knew that they were acting contrary to the blind people that sighted people usually had in mind. They were acting contrary to the "Stevie" look or the "Ray" look, as they called it.

"We have a view. I see," Bradley said.

All three of them laughed.

"Cool, man," Adam said. "We got a view. I think you're right, but I wonder what up with that?"

"Yeah, Hailey. I think we have a view too, but it's a little difficult to articulate."

"I know. I know," Hailey said. "What I mean— I mean it's not that you two don't see anything. Well, it's true you don't see anything—like, I mean you don't see all the tables in the bar and the windows back there behind you and the view from the window. You don't see that stuff. But I just don't think...I just can't believe that you don't see *some*thing."

"I think," Bradley said, "there's a difference between 'a view' and 'having a view.'"

"Something like that...something like that! What I mean—it's something like that. You two don't see anything and yet you see everything. This is what I mean. It's a paradox or a contradiction, I guess."

"But you know what I think?" Adam said.

"What?"

"Okay, here's the dealio. Here's what it is. People wit' eyeballs sometimes think—sometimes they think that we profound ones have a second sight or insight. They think we can see shit they don't. We can see inside the soul! We can see the real soul, not just of people but of everything. We got some kinda special gift! It's kinda like...it's kinda like.... Me. I'm the kinda dude—I'm the guy who got insight and second sight. And I got rhythm too."

All three laughed. They then clinked glasses in celebration of collective understanding.

"Where are you, man? Where are you? Let's clink."

"Yeah, Adam," Bradley said. "Let's clink and not spill this fucking beer on each other."

"Yeah. Comin' atcha, man. Chest level."

Clink.

"There we go. We got it done."

"All right...all right...."

"Got it. We cool."

Both of them then turned their gaze across the

table to Hailey, their pints of beer suspended in the air, very still.

"Hailey?"

Clink.

"Gotcha, man," she said.

"We good. We cool."

"At least I got one of them," Bradley said. "I got insight!"

They all laughed again.

"Yeah. But you and me dude, so you good," Adam said, laughing.

"So, what about me? What about me?" Hailey said, still laughing. "I got neither, so does that mean I got nothin'?"

"No. You got the intellect, the brains," Bradley said.

"Yeah," Adam said. "You got the iiiiintelllllect."

They all broke out into laughter for a few moments, not speaking but laughing gently and knowingly. They were looking at one another, or so it seemed. Their laughter flowed gently onto the shores of their awareness, almost mimicking the soothing sound of the gentle waves rising onto the shore from English Bay, at the edge of which the hotel was located.

"So, you figure that there's a difference between 'a view' and 'having a view'?" Bradley said. The individual waves of their awareness ebbed and flowed together.

"I think so," Hailey said. "It has to—I mean, they have to be different. You know, it's something like this, I guess. There's a view. It's outside of you. You see it; you sense it. And then there's *our* view *of* the view."

"Yeah. It's true. It's true. Okay, if I have a view—let's say I have a view, then Adam too maybe—if we have a view on the view, we must have the view."

They all laughed again.

"Can you be more vague?" Hailey laughed.

"Yeah, yeah, yeah. I can be more vague," Bradley said, laughing. "To have a view," he continued, "you must have a point of view, you have to have a view on some thing. So you can have a view—well, a point of view, actually, on politics, religion, yadda, yadda, yadda. Now that's true whether we—whether we're profoundly blind or not. But to have *the* view, see...that's a little different."

"This view is fucking amazing!" one of them said.

"This is really something else, man!" said another.

"This view is fucking great!" still another said.

They all stood at the rail of the balcony, admiring the view—all but him, he who sat on a deck chair, smoking and drinking his light beer.

"This is really amazing!" one of them said. "You guys are really lucky!"

Lucky, he thought as he took another sip of his beer. *Yeah...I'm really lucky.*

The three of them stood at the rail of the

balcony. They were looking south toward Lake Ontario. Before them stretched the city. Toronto spread itself out, below them, above them. They saw the view from the eighth-floor balcony. The view. Toronto. An enormous open-air cave spread before them and surrounded them, enclosing them in the view.

The sounds of the view spread over them as well; it embraced all of them, not only those standing at the rail, looking, but also him, he who sat on the deck chair, not looking. The sounds danced before them and around them. It came in waves, palpable. To those at the rail, the sounds were simply "city noise." To him, though, the sounds *were* the view. They were *his* view.

"I really love this view!" one of them said.

"What do you see?" he said.

"The whole thing! You can see—you can see all the way. The CN tower. And you can even see part of the lake."

"What are you looking at?" he said.

"Everything! It's just building after building. To the left, you can see U of T. You know, like, Robarts. Then you've got all these tall buildings, and they're spread out, like, in a pattern. Right—if you look right, it's all different. There's the Annex. You know, the residential streets. It's all green! You can see all the trees—all the trees lining the streets."

"Yeah, but what are you *looking* at?" he repeated.

"I'm looking at everything. You know, it's just,

like, you know, it's, like, the view. I'm looking at the view. Be right back. I'm going to go in and get my phone."

He sat in his chair, smoking, holding his can of beer. "So...so now he's going to get the view to stand still!" he said. "Stand still, view!"

"I'm back. It's so beautiful. I'm gonna get a pic and upload it to Instagram. Hashtag: view! Hashtag: Toronto! Hashtag: cityscape!"

"Yeah, I kinda remember," he said. "I kinda remember. It is beautiful. It is a beautiful view."

"You get the sounds, right? They must tell you something, right?"

"That's my deal, man. The sounds. That's my gig. Sounds. That's how the view shows itself to me."

"That's cool. I guess the sounds orient you. Or does all this noise just confuse you?"

"No," he said. "The sounds come right up off that street, right to me. Well, right to all of us. Streetcars, traffic, sirens, people talking on the street. It comes right up here! And somethin' has to be makin' those sounds. It's, like, somethin' had to make that view."

He sat, sipping his beer, and wondered whether the view would be amazing without sound. The idea of deafness came to him and, with the sounds of the street, mingled in with his thoughts. *The view* would *be amazing to a deaf person*, he thought, just as it was to him.

But the sounds—the sounds were the key to the view for him. The city buildings, the cars, the streetcars—all of these things. All of them were silent until people made them speak. The city came alive in the lives of people. He smiled as he thought these things. *The view. There it is. That's the view. The life of the city.* That's *the amazing view*, he mused. The city was born and will live forever. It will live as long as the tragedy and comedy known as human life does.

"You guys are right," he said. "The view *is* amazing!"

"True. We can describe it to you and then it's amazing to you too," one of them said.

"Yeah. And now if you could just try to listen to what you see.... If you could only hear the view."

"I know what you mean," Hailey said. "Like I said before, we see a view. I mean, *the* view." She laughed. "But like I said before, we see a view. We sense a view. Aaaaand you and Adam, the two of you, sense a view. So you have *the* view."

"Yeah."

"So...so...so we have *the* view," Adam said.

"Right. You two have, uhhh, the view."

"We do. We do. We do," Bradley said.

Laughing, Adam said, "True dat! We see things. There's stuff here. There's the tables, the chairs, all around the bar. There's the bar, the server, walls, the floor. We know all that. We see the floor, the table here, the chairs, the stools we're sitting on."

"And we have a view on that view, right?"

Bradley said.

"True! True! Cozy, not cozy. Comfortable. Good feel. Good feel in the room. We feel all that. That's our view of the view."

"But you have something more, or different, in mind, don't you Hailey?" Bradley said.

"Yeah, sort of. But, I mean, uh, I mean...."

All three were quiet again. And again it seemed as though they were all looking at one another. This time, though, Hailey looked in a way very similar to how the other two looked. All three looked in that particular way, giving life to a genuine care. Their look was a look of generosity. Their look invited each other to speak. It was generous in its listening.

"Okay! Okay! Let me—I want..." Hailey said. "Okay! This is it, I think. Okay. Okay, behind you two, behind your backs, is English Bay. English Bay is the background. There's huge, big windows behind your backs too. English Bay is facing me. I can see it! I can see it. It's beautiful. It's a great view!

"So..." she continued, "so what a great view. What does this mean? Something like this. We see things, right? But...but...some things we see. Some things we call a view. Everything is not a view, or the view. Okay, like this. There's English Bay, right? A great view, right? But there's Beach Avenue right in front of it. I mean, I can see Beach Avenue too, which I see first, then I see English Bay. But I didn't say, 'Oh, there's Beach Avenue. What an amazing view!' No, I said,

'English Bay. What an amazing view!' So...."

"No. Exactly. Exactly," Adam said. "C'mon, man. This is all that philosophy stuff you guys talk. C'mon, man. Jam in. Help me out."

"Help you out? Help you out...? *You're* the artist, man. You got the *im-ag-o-na-tion*."

"We got dat too...'cause we blind!"

They all laughed again. This time, though, Hailey's laugh wasn't as exuberant.

Just then, their server approached their table. "How are we doing here? Another round?"

"I think so," Hailey said. "What do you guys think? I think. Yeah. Another round."

The server smiled. He looked at Bradley and Adam and then at Hailey. After a quick return look to the server, Hailey turned her look to the two of them. In the silence, there was almost a question asked.

"Great!" the server said finally. "Another lager, another ale. And your red was the, uh...."

"The Malbec."

"Malbec. Right. Back in a sec."

"We're the only ones here," Hailey said. "What time is it, I wonder?"

Bradley pressed a button on his wristwatch. The watch spoke in its computer voice: *Eleven—fifty-eight—p.m.*

"Almost midnight," Adam said. "No one else here? Just us?"

"Nope! Just us."

"It *is* only a Wednesday," Bradley said.

"Yeah. That's true," Hailey said.

They were silent for a few moments. The bar was almost as silent as they were. The low tones of someone speaking in the reception area of the hotel just beyond the bar; the background thrum of what sounded like a refrigerator at the bar about thirty feet away; the sound of glasses clinking came from the same area. In the momentary silence, these were the sounds they could hear.

Bradley's left hand rested on his cheek. He wondered about this amazing view, English Bay. He imagined its beauty, and *he knew* it was amazing.

He sat now, his left cheek in his hand, his fingers curled. Many years ago—*too many*, he thought—he could see. Not much, but a little. He lived in Vancouver back then, where he could see the amazing view of English Bay. He didn't see what others saw, he knew. They saw it all—all of its beauty. He didn't. He saw a little of it. He smiled a little now as he contemplated "seeing a little." *What did that mean?* he wondered. Is it possible to see "a little" beauty? Bradley wondered if people "with eyeballs," as Adam often called people who could see, could see all the beauty instead of just a little of it as he could.... Well, as he used to. What could he and Adam see? What do "the profoundly blind" see when they look at the amazing view of English Bay? All of these questions streamed in his mind as he sat on the bar stool, smiling.

"What are you smiling at?" Hailey said.

"I was wondering about English Bay. Beautiful, an amazing view! I know. I used to be able to see it a little bit a long time ago, in my ten percent days. The ocean, the mountains in the background, this beautiful beach—all that stuff. I remember. Is that beach still beautiful, Hailey? Still all that gorgeous sand? The sea wall? Is it?"

"The funny thing is I want to say yes. The beach is still beautiful. The funny thing is, though, I'm looking out the window at English Bay, and I can't see it in this darkness! I see a few lights across where the university is, but I can't see the view! But I know it's beautiful and amazing! I can't see it right now. But I know."

"Ohhhhh-kayyyyy. Here's your ale at twelve o'clock. And your lager at twelve o'clock. Aaaaand a glass of Malbec. Enjoy. Cheers."

They said their thanks, and the silence resumed when the server left once again. Adam broke it this time.

"You do remember what it looks like. You saw it earlier. So...so you know it's beautiful. You know it's an amazing view."

"Right."

"But, at the same time, you *can* see it. You know it's an amazing view because you remember seeing it. It *is* there. But you can't see it right now. It's in the dark. You're seeing an amazing view in the dark! There's something cool about that."

Once more, they sat in silence, Bradley and Adam drinking from their pints, Hailey sipping her wine. Once more, Adam broke the silence.

"So, but, so...you not in the dark like us. 'Cause we not in the dark, right, man?"

"No. No. You're right. I've got all the millions of little coloured lights moving, shaking, twinkling all the time. And you've got those colours too, man, right? What do you call these lights in that play you wrote, Adam?"

"Mental canvas."

"Right. Mental canvas. We've each got a mental canvas."

"And...we paintin' on 'em. We constantly paintin' on 'em."

Hailey's eyes opened wide. "You're right.... You're right!" she exclaimed. She moved her hands enthusiastically in the way she did when she spoke. "You two, both of you, you have a mental canvas. This is good. This is really good! You paint on this canvas. And this is the cool thing. Your paint and your brushes are, well, your imaginations! You paint with your imagination."

"Yeah, in a sense, that's what we do," Bradley said. "What we do is paint images—images like 'the *view*'—with our imaginations. We paint images with our imaginations on this imaginary mental canvas. We're just *full* of imagination, man."

"You're right, man," Adam said. "We really do that. The *view* comes to us, but it does so 'cause we paint it. We paint the view. Then it comes to us. But we also *bring* the view to ourselves in our imagination. It's funny.... It's funny. The *view* comes to us because we bring it."

"You too, Hailey," Bradley said. "The amazing view of English Bay is coming to you now, in the dark, because you're bringing it to yourself in your imagination."

More silence. Hailey looked at the two of them as they sat quietly, slowly drinking from their pints of beer. Finally, she spoke.

"It's true...it's true. The three of us have a mental canvas. Yours is different somehow—different from mine—but we all have a mental canvas. I'm sighted, and you guys are blind—"

"Profoundly blind!" Adam interrupted, laughing.

"Right, *profoundly* blind," continued Hailey. "I'm sighted, and yet I have a mental canvas like you two."

"Now, see, that's *also* profound!" Bradley said.

"Yes," Hailey said. "Yes. Yes, it is profound. And I wonder—I wonder if that's what makes a *view*...makes a view a view? I mean, what is on our mental canvas when we call a view 'amazing'? It can't be the *view*, just the view that's amazing, just on its own. It has to be us too! It's not only the view."

"Wow. That's amazing!" Bradley said.

They sat in silence once more. They knew they were onto something, but they weren't sure exactly. And yet they knew that something amazing happened.

The server approached their table again and smiled. "Sorry, but this is last call. Would you like another round?"

"Oh, sorry," Hailey said. "We're the only ones left in here."

"That's okay," the server said. "You can have another round and just relax. What do you think?"

"Yeah? Yeah. One more and call it a night? Yeah. Good. Yeah, one more."

"What kinda bullshit you talkin'?" one of them said to him, laughing.

"Hey, man. What's up?" he said.

"Bullshit! What dat bullshit you sayin'?"

"What bullshit?"

"Tellin' me...hear da view, listen to da view. Dat! Bullshit."

Both of them were laughing now.

"Come on. What up wit' dat bullshit?"

"Well," he said, "you describe the view to me, then I can see it. Now that's bullshit."

"No, no, no. I don't need to listen to no goddamn view. I can see the motherfucker."

"Yeah. I can hear the motherfucker. If you listen, you can hear it and see it."

"Hey! You got the camera. Stand there. Take a picture of the motherfucker drinking dat lake water shit. It go to his head."

Laughing, he held his can of light beer up high, smiled, and said, "I hear that camera takin' a picture."

"Okay! Okay, here we go." The server put their drinks on the table in front of them. "Ale at twelve o'clock. Lager, twelve o'clock."

"Actually, it's about quarter *to* twelve," Bradley said, touching his fresh pint of beer and laughing as the server put Hailey's glass of Malbec in front of her.

The server then put the bill on the table, said that they should take their time, and with a "Cheers!" moved back behind the bar.

"Nice and quiet in here," Bradley said.

"Yeah. It is," Adam said. "We still the only ones in here, Hailey?"

"Yup, just the three of us. You're right. It's nice and quiet, but it's a little eerie, too."

Without speaking, the three of them nodded their heads.

"I gotta go pee," Hailey said. "Back shortly."

"Cheers! Cheers, my friend," Bradley said after she left. "Think we can do this?"

"We got this thing down," Adam said.

Clink! Their pints touched, and with a laugh they said, "Cheers!" to each other again and drank.

Both of them kept their right hands curled around their pints of beer. They spoke about that, wondering whether keeping their hands on their pints was a habit or a ritual. It wasn't likely a habit, they both concluded. Possibly a ritual. Yet, the ritual, if that's what it was, was born of the need to have their pints permanently located in their field of touch, a need they mutually shared.

They joked about how, more than once, a pint of beer was knocked over, or close to it, when it wasn't in their field of touch.

"So...so when I get up," Adam said, "say I get up to go to the can or something, I make sure my beer is pushed away, you know, further from my hand. So I don't smack it over when, you know, I stand up and lean over the table a little. Man, I learned to do that *real* quick."

"That's cool. I gotta start doin' that. I never knocked anything over so far, but I've come close a few times."

They then heard footsteps approach the table.

"Hailey?" Bradley said.

"Hey, Hailey...you back," Adam said, more of a statement than a question.

No words came to them from the end of the table, from the direction toward which they were both looking. There was no sound other than the footsteps they had both heard only a moment ago. They looked as though they were looking at one another, and doing so quizzically.

"Hailey? You there?" Bradley asked again.

"Y'all messin' wit' our *heads*?" Adam said.

"I heard fucking footsteps! I really did!"

"Me too, man! I heard them plain—plain!"

"I'm guessing that someone probably came into the bar and moved past us," Bradley said. "Only thing—only thing is I didn't hear the footsteps go past. They just stopped at the table right here beside me."

"Me too, man. Me too. I heard them come from those two steps there. You know, the ones goin' to the bathroom. And the footsteps—they just stopped right here, right at the table. Right here beside me!"

More footsteps.

"Hey, you guys. I'm back," Hailey said.

"Y'all bin messin' wit' us?" Adam said.

"*What?*"

"Messin' wit' us. You know, y'all bin messin' wit' us."

"Yeah. We heard you," Bradley said. "We heard you. We heard you come down those steps and walk over here to our table. And then nothin'... nothin'!"

"No! No! I just got back from the bathroom. Just now! Just now!"

"You serious?" Bradley said.

"Yeah! Just now! I just got back. Really. Honest."

"So...so...you...you see anyone else in the bar now?" Adam said.

"No. Just us. Just us three," Hailey said.

"That's fuckin' weird, man," Adam said.

"Man!" Bradley said. "Man. Hailey, I mean—I mean, we *heard* them. *Footsteps!* Footsteps coming right from those steps, right up to the table. Right up to the table. They came right up here, right to the end of the table. Right here, right beside me. I know. It's weird. Adam and I said, 'Hey, Hailey, that you?'"

"And nuttin'! Nuttin'!" Adam said. "The steps...they just come right up here and stop. And then nuttin'! We sayin', 'Hailey. Hey, Hailey, that you?' Nuttin'! Then we hear more footsteps comin' from those two steps there and then...*you* here at the table."

"Yeah, man! Footsteps! Footsteps! Heard 'em! Right here! Footsteps! That wasn't *you*? We heard you. We thought it was you!"

All of these words came in a rush and seemed to emanate from both of them simultaneously. It was choreographed sound! It was the sound of sheer disbelief! Remarkably, their right hands remained curled around their pints of beer even as their left hands were moving rapidly through the field of touch that surrounded them.

"I don't know what the fuck is going on!" Bradley said. "There's gotta be someone else in this bar besides us! Someone musta come in!"

"No!" Hailey said. "There's no one else here. Honest! It's just us."

They sat, not speaking. The hushed sounds of the bar surrounded them—the hum of a refrigerator; the quiet murmur of a ventilation fan; the distant sound of coins clinking as the bartender counted the night's take. No steps, though. Someone walking was not part of the soundscape that surrounded them in their silence.

"Well," Hailey said, her voice hushed with the sound of finality, "looks like we're all done."

"The bill?" Bradley said.

"Oh, yeah," Hailey said. "I'm gonna use cash."

"You need…" Adam said.

"It's good." Hailey said. "I got it."

"That was a great night," Bradley said. "And to top it all off, we heard steps, Adam. Steps. No person."

"Yeah, man. We done heard steps. Nobody make 'em, those steps. Just steps."

"I know!" Hailey said. "You guys saw a *ghost*."

"Must be," Bradley said.

"Gots to be," Adam said. "What else? We saw ourselves a *ghost*."

Adam and Bradley laughed as they stood, pushing their bar stools in toward the table.

"Excuse me," Bradley said, turning his look toward the bar. "Cash for the bill on the table here."

"Thanks. Have a good night."

"You two blind guys saw a ghost!" Hailey said, "Un*fucking*believable! You two, *the* view. And now a ghost! That's an amazing view!"

Hailey moved around the table to join them. Bradley took Hailey's right arm, and Adam gently held onto his shoulder. They all said thanks to the bartender and, three wide, moved to the two steps that led out of the bar.

They were moving indoors now. They decided to eat inside rather than bring their plates, heaped with food, onto the balcony.

They would return to the amazing view later.

He followed the others, closing the balcony door behind him, shutting out the amazing view. The view could still grasp the attention of the others, though. Coming through the wall of windows that separated the apartment from the balcony, the view spread itself over them, touching them. It beckoned their eyes with its touch and awaited their look of amazement.

He had the fragrance and the sound of the view in him. It floated through him, touching him. The view did not beckon him, though. He did not need a window. The view did not need to attract his attention. His attention and the view circled one another and came together in the commingling of touch that made the view—any view—amazing.

Things Are Different Here

Bradley was becoming a little more accustomed to the unusual flow of traffic. The flow was opposite to that of Toronto, where he lived. But this was Manchester. Things were different here. The driver's seat was on the opposite side. So different from what he was accustomed to. And the drivers drove on the wrong side—the wrong side!

Bradley was slowly becoming accustomed to these differences. This was, after all, his third trip to Manchester in the past four years. The last time he was in Manchester was two years ago. He and Hailey had spent two months living in the Northern Quarter during their sabbatical from the University of Toronto. And, now, here they were, back for a month this time.

Bradley stood there, on Thomas Street, waiting for Hailey. She had gone into a shop. This was another thing about Manchester. Here, stores were called "shops." Hailey was in one of these shops now, one that sold jewelry.

He felt this disorientation now as he stood at the curb, facing Thomas Street. Except for one-way streets back home, cars always approached from the left. Here in Manchester, though, it was the opposite—cars came from the right. Listening to the left was a habitual practice for Bradley. Listening to the right? That was a different matter.

"Hey, Bradley," Hailey said as she approached him.

"Hailey."

"What are you doing standing alone at the curb?"

"Just checking it out. Checking it out."

"I know what you mean," Hailey told him. "It's confusing. But I think I'm getting a little used to looking to the right for the traffic coming at me."

"Yeah. I still find it a little weird. Anyway, did you get anything in that craft shop?"

"No. But they had some great rings."

"Did you get one?"

"I didn't like any of them. They didn't really suit me."

"I thought you said they had some great rings in there."

"Yeah. No. I meant for *you*, Bradley. I think you'd really like them. They were kinda big and, uh, sorta heavy-looking."

"So, there's rings that I would like but none that you would like."

"Yup."

"See, Hailey, that's what you're always like."

"Like what? What do you mean?"

"You never buy anything."

"Yes, I do."

"But you have to look at a hundred places, like a hundred ring stores."

"Shops. Ring *shops*."

"Right. Right. Shops. Hailey, you'd have to look at every single ring in the Northern Quarter before you'd pick one out. Same as you do with everything else. Like the jeans you bought. You had to look everywhere in the Northern Quarter and even in Deansgate before you went back to Selfridges, where, *by the way*, you began looking for jeans, and then you bought them there."

"I know. But I'll get a ring. You'll see, Bradley. I think we should go back in there and pick out a ring for you."

"I don't feel like it right now. Let's have a coffee first and then walk to Deansgate."

"Are you sure?"

"Yeah."

"You wanna walk?"

"I like the Odd. Don't you?"

"It's not bad. It's not my favourite bar. But it's not bad."

"You like the English Lounge, right, Bradley?"

"Yeah. They make better Americanos there. But these aren't bad."

"Plus we get to sit outside. And you can smoke. I really like sitting out here, right on Thomas Street. I like watching what's going on."

Bradley and Hailey sat on the patio directly across the street from the ring shop. It was a great day, sunny and even warm by Manchester standards. Bradley sat across from Hailey. He was relaxed. Drinking an Americano, smoking a cigarette, and talking to Hailey while listening to the sounds of Thomas Street here in the Northern Quarter was great. *What could be better*? he thought.

"So, you wanna go to Deansgate, hey?"

"Yeah, Hailey. I wanna check out some boots. I'd like to get some boots. Remember that boot store the last time we were here?"

"Oh, right," Hailey said. "I can't remember the name of it right now."

"Me neither. But it'll come to me. Plus you'll recognize it when we see it."

"That's true."

"Maybe we can both get boots."

"Maybe. We'll see."

They fell silent, and Bradley turned his attention to the voices, those accents he enjoyed so much. He listened to people speaking as they walked by on Thomas Street, and then his ear caught a conversation taking place on the patio at a table directly behind him. To him it sounded like two people. But if there were more, they weren't speaking. They were having an argument. Not a fight, exactly, but a disagreement.

A man and a woman. Two people. Two of them, Bradley was certain now. There were two people.

He could make out some of what they were saying, enough to pick up the gist of their disagreement. Something about a Jacuzzi in the bath. She wanted one. He didn't.

A Jacuzzi was too posh, he was telling her.

"Bollocks," she said. "I'm not too posh."

"Not you. The *Jacuzzi* is posh," he corrected himself.

She insisted that she wanted a Jacuzzi and that it wasn't too posh and neither was she. He insisted that he didn't say she was too posh.

"The Jacuzzi. *The Jacuzzi.* That's what's too posh, not you."

She stood her ground. "It's not right that you're calling me posh. You shouldn't do that."

"To be fair, I said the *Jacuzzi* is posh, *not you!* Not you. The Jacuzzi."

She insisted that it was the same thing. If the Jacuzzi is too posh and she wanted one in her bath, "Then it stands to reason," she said, "that I'm too posh, too."

"Rubbish," he said. "I'm just takin' the piss."

Hailey's words interrupted Bradley's eavesdropping. "What do you think? Another Americano? Or should we just go?"

"I think...yeah, I think one more Americano. How about you?"

"Yeah. I'm gonna go in and order them."

"Great," Bradley said.

"Okay. Leaving the table now."

Just then, Bradley heard the scraping of chairs behind him. The couple was leaving. "Damn!" he said.

What! What was that...? There! Again! Was that...was that a flash?

Bradley was standing outside the House of Fraser, a department store in Deansgate, when he saw what he thought was a flash coming somewhere from his left. He was leaning against the wall of the store, smoking his cigarette and waiting for Hailey. She had gone inside to look at scarves. "I'll just be a few minutes. They're on the main floor. I'll just be a few minutes."

He stood there now, leaning against the wall, smoking to calm himself. For years, Bradley hadn't seen anything, and now this—a flash of light. Tiny, shimmering, brightly coloured lights had completely filled his eyes for decades now. No flashes of lights. Just coloured lights. These lights were like a barrier, like a barricade really. They barricaded Bradley from the world. They kept the world at bay. The world couldn't get in. The lights made sure of that.

All wasn't lost, though. Some of the world did get in. He could hear it. Smell it. And he could even touch it, from time to time. Add to this what people told him, and what he remembered from when he could see, and Bradley had a sense of the world. But for the most part, those lights, those zillions of bright, shimmering, coloured lights, kept the world out and...kept him in.

But now, in front of the House of Fraser, something was getting in. Bradley stubbed his cigarette out on the wall behind him and let it drop to the pavement. He lit another one.

He was a little shaken by what he saw or by what he thought he saw. It couldn't have been a flash from outside of his eyes, he thought. It sure did look like it though. A bright flash of light coming from his left.

There! Again! A flash. Definitely a flash of light coming from his left. This time, though...this flash lasted longer than the first one did.

Bradley turned quickly to his left, trying to capture the light. *Where is it? I saw it. I know I did.* Now it was gone. Gone. Gone. Gone.

Turn. Walk toward it. It had to be there. Bradley saw it. *Walk. Slowly. You will run into it.*

Not so bad, Bradley thought, as he made his way in the direction from which he and Hailey had come.

Down Deansgate to Bridge Street. Two, maybe three blocks. Bradley couldn't remember. But he thought he would recognize the sound of Bridge Street as it intersected Deansgate.

Nice sidewalk, Bradley thought as he slowly made his way. *Not sidewalk*, he reminded himself. *"Pavement."* This was Manchester, and things were different here.

The pavement was narrow, not like those wide sidewalks back home in Toronto. *Better*, Bradley thought. Much easier to stay oriented and walk in a straight line. Put your white stick out to the right a little, and there—the curb; to the left, and there—a building or a pavement café. In Toronto, though, things were different. Walking a straight line on the sidewalk was much more difficult. It could take four steps to find a curb or a building. Here in Manchester, things were different. *Much, much better*, Bradley thought.

Bridge Street and Deansgate. These streets didn't cross as streets do back home, Bradley tried to remember. It wasn't a square intersection, he thought. There was something weird about it. The streets were somehow circular. *Okay*, he thought. *It'll be okay. There's always someone to ask.*

There! Again! The light. This time, though, not exactly a flash—the light stayed on much longer. *Straight. Go straight.* Bradley urged himself on toward the light.

The light was back. Not a flash this time, but a beam, a steady illumination. No flashes, just white illumination. Bradley urged himself on.

Was it far? Was it near? He couldn't tell. He wasn't sure if he was headed for it or walking in it. It was bright.

Funny though, Bradley thought. He couldn't see anything. All this light, and he couldn't see a thing. All this light.

It was becoming more difficult for him to walk.

His pace began to slow. His white stick was moving in that familiar left-to-right, right-to-left rhythm. It was moving a little slower than usual, but it was still conducting itself in the usual manner. So long as his white stick was doing so, Bradley felt he would be okay and could keep going—a little slower, but he could keep going.

No longer flashing and so constant, the damn light *was* distracting. It was very bright. But not like daylight. Bradley remembered what it was like, back then. He remembered daylight. This was not like that. It was all *light*. Nothing was distinct. There were no shapes that he could imagine. His brightly coloured lights were gone, too. Nothing. Just light. Bright, bright light.

Bradley wondered whether he was still headed toward Bridge Street. He couldn't tell. He started in that direction, but now he wasn't sure. He was walking straight. At least, he thought he was. But in what direction?

His white stick wasn't coming into contact with anything. It wasn't hitting anything on the pavement, not posts, not newspaper stands, not anything. *Am I on the pavement?* he wondered. *That light. Can't see. Can't tell.* Bradley's anxiety got higher.

Bradley was no longer curious about the light. He no longer cared. He wanted *out* of it. He hated it. It frightened him.

Then...Hailey. He remembered that he was waiting for her. *Is she still in the House of Fraser? Where is she?* He was more frightened than ever now. He turned. He concentrated, trying to make an exact 180-degree turn. There were no landmarks, nothing to orient him. He wanted to turn from the light and make his way into the store, back to Hailey.

Slowly, he turned. Light! All light! Bradley wondered if he had turned enough. Did he turn 180 degrees? His back should be to the light. Brightly coloured lights, his light—that's what should be in front of him...if he turned 180 degrees.

Bradley stopped and swept his cane from left to right, side to side, on what he thought was the pavement. Nothing. His white stick hit nothing. Nothing on the pavement. No brightly coloured lights. Just *light*...surrounding him, preventing him from.... *From what?* he wondered.

He shouted Hailey's name.

Then he screamed it. "*HAILEY!*"

Bradley couldn't believe his ears. He screamed Hailey's name but didn't hear his own scream. He tried again. Nothing. It was as though the sound of his scream evaporated because of the light. There was nothing.

Bradley braced himself and slowly moved into the bright light. Nothing was familiar to him. His own brightly coloured lights were gone. He didn't know whether he was on the pavement or whether he was moving back to where he was originally standing, waiting for Hailey. There was one familiar thing, though: his white stick. It resumed its customary left-to-right, right-to-left movement as he walked. Bradley found comfort in that.

And then there it was. His white stick hit it first. Solid. A wall. Bradley stopped and turned to face the wall. He extended his left arm and touched it. He turned and leaned against the wall. He breathed deeply. He would worry about things later. *First, regain my calm.*

Bradley reached into the pocket of his leather jacket and retrieved his pack of cigarettes. He removed one, replaced the pack, and began fumbling in the pocket of his jeans for his lighter. *Got it.* Bradley lit his cigarette, inhaled deeply, and leaned back against the wall, white stick in his right hand, cigarette in his left. *Time to take stock.*

He leaned against the wall. He moved his shoulders from side to side, trying to discern the nature of the surface of the wall. He did the same with his left foot, bending his knee, touching the wall. He touched the wall with his left hand, the one that held his cigarette. Was this the House of Fraser? Was this the wall against which he was leaning before he began to chase the light? *It feels like the same wall*, he thought. *That stonework.* He thought he felt the stonework that Hailey had said she liked. She had actually made him touch it so that he could see how different things were, here in Manchester. Bradley thought he was feeling that same stonework now.

No Hailey. She wasn't there, outside of the House of Fraser, waiting for him. She would have said something if she was. *That's good*, Bradley thought. Hailey wasn't wondering where he was. *She's still inside, looking for a scarf.* He wasn't certain of this, though. It did seem as though he had been looking for that light for quite some time, more than just a few minutes, he thought. He wasn't certain either that the wall he was now leaning against was that of the House of Fraser. It felt like it was, but he couldn't be sure. *Oh, well,* Bradley thought, *it is what it is. Gotta go with what I know. That's all I know.*

Bradley inhaled deeply. *My lighter—what did I do with my lighter?* The cigarette was in his left hand, the white stick in his right. *No lighter. I must have put it back in my pocket*, he reasoned.

He took one more drag from his cigarette and, like before, stubbed it out on the wall behind him and let it drop to the pavement. He moved his left hand down his body to the pocket of his jeans to see if he could feel his lighter. *There. I must have put it back.*

All these rips on my jeans—they go all the way down to the knee. I like the feel. Bradley liked the fact that rips and tears in jeans were in fashion.

What did they call them? Oh, yeah. Distressed. He smiled at this. *Distressed*, he thought. *How bougie. Not "ripped" but "distressed."* He remembered what a friend had once said about his distressed jeans: "Nice jeans. Gotta love those designer holes." He remembered another time, the time that he felt the back pocket of his jeans and discovered that the Armani emblem was missing. "Damn. I lost the Armani sign!" he'd said. "I guess," his friend replied, "your jeans are just jeans now."

Still, Bradley liked the feel of the rips and tears in his jeans, artificial as they were. He liked them because they reminded him of a long time ago when he was a teenager. A rip or a tear in your jeans back then resulted in nothing but embarrassment, especially when you had nothing else to wear. Rips were a different kind of distress then. Now, though, you pay for them, and you pay a lot.

He continued to touch the designer rips and tears. He was in touch with his jeans. It was almost as though he had regained his sight.

Bradley lit another cigarette. He leaned against the wall (of what he hoped was the House of Fraser) and pondered his next move. The light was still there—very bright, enveloping him. There was nothing else. No point chasing it. It was there. In fact, it seemed to Bradley that it was everywhere. He thought he might head straight and see if he could hit the curb. This would let him know if the street, Deansgate, was still there. He knew it was. But he thought maybe he should find out.

It then occurred to him that the light might be inside the House of Fraser. It may have penetrated the walls and moved inside. *Maybe*, Bradley thought, *I should try to find the door and see whether the light is inside*. He thought maybe he would do this after he found the curb.

Suddenly, Bradley stubbed his cigarette out on the wall behind him and dropped it to the pavement. He had made up his mind. Forget finding the curb. He was headed into the House of Fraser. He would find out if the light were in there.

He turned and followed the wall to his left where he remembered the door had been. Sure enough, there it was. A few steps and, with his hand, he felt the glass curve that indicated the revolving door. He felt good. This *was* the House of Fraser. He *had been* leaning against its wall, smoking.

Hailey hated these doors, he remembered. She said it was too difficult for her to describe them to him. She always thought he would get hurt, and this made her anxious. It was too ridiculous, she always said. It was ridiculous to guide a blind person through these "spinning doors," as she sometimes called them. In fact, Hailey called them everything *but* revolving doors. *What did she call them the last time?* Bradley wondered. *Oh, right. Rotisserie doors. She actually called them "rotis-*

serie doors." He located one of the panels of the rotisserie door. He set his jaw against the door and pushed.

The light didn't surprise Bradley as it had the first time. Somehow he knew it would be there. And he felt more afraid than surprised. Nothing he could do about it though. It was there. And it was bright. He had hoped, *really* hoped, that the bright light wouldn't be there, inside the House of Fraser, but it was. And somehow he knew it would be.

The light had penetrated the walls of the House of Fraser and made its way inside. Bradley could see this at the very moment the movement of the revolving door had deposited him inside. He was inside, wasn't he? This was the House of Fraser, wasn't it? No difference—at least none that he could detect. Bright outside; bright inside. But the door did move. It moved in that circular fashion so familiar to him. It was a revolving door, after all. *Although, with all this intense bright light, 'rotisserie door' might be a more apt name for it*, Bradley thought. Still, it was a door. Doors do move you from inside to outside and vice versa. This must be true now. Things can't be that different here in Manchester. Bradley did feel the wall outside. He did lean against it and smoke a couple of cigarettes. He did feel the revolving door, and he did pass through it. He must be inside.

The best thing to do, Bradley reasoned, was to

move forward a few steps and then move to the right. He remembered that the scarves were *there* when he and Hailey were here in the House of Fraser a few days ago—a few steps from the front door and then to the right. He would go there now and find the scarves. He knew that if he found the scarves, he would find Hailey. He was, though, hoping that Hailey would see him or have already seen him coming in through the revolving door.

Bradley began moving forward. His white stick told him that the surface was different. It was different from the surface on the other side of the revolving door. Maybe, he thought, he really was inside. Still, no Hailey and no racks of scarves.

A thought made him stop dead in his tracks. Its terror was as palpable as the bright light. *What if—just what if—the bright light prevented Hailey from seeing? What if it prevented anyone from seeing? What if it prevented seeing?*

Bradley couldn't move.

Get outside. Turn—180 degrees—then find the revolving door. Get. Out. Bradley couldn't think of anything else. What else could he do? *Get outside. Find the wall. Have a smoke. Get calm. Then...then....*

Bradley stood, concentrating. Just like he did when he was outside in the bright light, he concentrated now. He had to make an exact 180-degree turn. This would get him back to the revolving door and back outside. All he wanted was his brightly coloured lights. He wanted, desperately wanted, them back. They were his. This bright light wasn't. Bradley didn't know to whom this bright light belonged. It wasn't his, though.

Get out! Get out! Get outside!

Bradley screamed, "*HAILEY!*" He heard nothing.

CPSIA information can be obtained
at www.ICGtesting.com
Printed in the USA
LVOW03s0239130717
541188LV00004B/6/P

Things Are Different Here